HOLIDAY MAGIC
THE GIFT OF LOVE

LAURIE RYAN

LAVADA DEE

Enjoy the season,
Laurie Ryan

HEALING LOVE
by Laurie Ryan

1

Nicole Milbourne leaned in with a gloved hand to swab the patient's hive-covered leg for yet another culture. It shouldn't be this hard to diagnose a simple rash. Red blotches admittedly covered fifty percent of the patient's legs, so Nicole corrected her assessment. Maybe it wasn't so simple.

"Ouch."

The sound startled Nicole and the applicator flew out of her hand, settling with a soft thunk on the floor.

Nicole glanced at the portly woman she'd been assigned to follow up on. The head of the hospital bed was raised and the woman peered over her glasses at Nicole, her arms folded across her chest. With her lips set in a thin line of censure, it didn't take a body language expert to determine the woman's mindset.

"I'm sorry," Nicole said. "I didn't expect it would hurt."

"Well, it did," the woman answered. Her artificially carrot-colored hair didn't budge as she bobbed her head up and down.

Nicole tried to smile, certain it looked more like a jerky group of still frames end to end than a natural gesture of friendliness. If she couldn't carry on an ordinary conversation like this with a patient, how was she ever going to survive the residency program?

She reached for another swab kit.

"You're doing another culture?"

"Yes," Nicole said, focused on opening the stubborn paper and space-age plastic packet.

"Why?"

"It's possible we cultured too soon and the infection hadn't really taken hold, even though the symptoms were manifesting themselves."

The quiet whoosh of the hospital room door startled Nicole and the swab in her hand went spiraling to the floor. With a sigh, she reached for a third kit, quite certain it was going to be a very long three years.

Glancing up, her heart skipped about ten beats when her worst fears came true and the head resident walked in to the room.

Dr. Damien Reed was a legend in the halls of Rochester Regional. With an impressive scholastic resume', Kennedy looks, and a smile that could disarm the Middle East, the man was both respected by his peers and ogled by just about every woman in the place.

From a resident's perspective, that smile meant a thorough textbook grilling generally followed, which explained the pounding heart syndrome she got when she spotted him in the hallways.

Nicole had managed to escape his notice for her entire first week...almost. She clutched the swab kit. Today was day six of her residency.

She offered him a quick, professional nod and prayed he wouldn't ask her any questions. After taking a long moment scrutinizing her, he turned his charms on his patient. Nicole exhaled relief as she watched him interact with the woman.

"Mrs. O'Malley," he said with a wide grin as he held her hand between his and dug up some bad Irish charm. "And how are we doing this fine morning?"

As usual, Dr. Reed's dark hair was unkempt and shaggy. Nicole reached up to touch her own auburn hair, neatly captured in a bun at the nape of her neck, then remembered her gloved hands and dropped them to her side. The man's hair was reminiscent of a college student, not someone who'd risen to the position that put him in charge of newly indoctrinated medical residents. She tried to ignore jeans that fit too well, yet seemed completely inappropriate for someone with his status. This was Rochester Regional Medical Center, after all. There were protocols to be observed.

She studied him as he spoke with the patient and the conversation faded to gray. Even inappropriate, the hairstyle worked for him, framing a strong face, green eyes, and an effortless smile. No one appeared immune to his easy charm, least of all Mrs. O'Malley.

With the personality of a politician, everything seemed easy for Dr. Damien Reed. Not so for herself. A part of her envied him those skills.

Nicole yanked open another swab kit, surprised when it came apart in one pull and almost went flying again. When Dr. Reed's steady hands grasped hers as well as the kit, she chalked the slight quake in her arms up to first week nerves. If he held on longer than necessary, Nicole decided it had been to keep the swab from falling to the floor.

Nicole mumbled a thank you as Dr. Reed held out the swab for her to take.

"Anytime." Even the man's voice was designed for effect. The single word rolled off his tongue like warm honey. She could understand why patients sought him out. He made everything seem better with a simple word.

As Mrs. O'Malley ran down her list of complaints to Dr. Reed, Nicole, with extreme care this time, swabbed the rash, and then pulled the blanket back over the patient's leg.

"Thank you, dear. That was much better," Mrs. O'Malley said. "She was a bit rough on the first try," the patient explained to Dr. Reed, sending Nicole's already pink complexion into overdrive, if the warmth of her face was any indication. The man had the power to toss her out of the program with little or no reason, but he simply patted Mrs. O'Malley's hand and turned to Nicole.

For a moment, he held her gaze. When Nicole realized her lips were parted, she clamped them shut. Irritation replaced nerves when she watched his eyebrow lift in response.

"How are we on bringing this rash of Mrs. O'Malley's under control?"

Nicole took a deep breath. She would not be escaping his infamous grilling today, it appeared. Taking a moment, she reminded herself that this was where she excelled. She knew her diseases and what needed to be done to diagnose them. No one in the residency program would best her at diagnostic medicine. It was her strong point, as she'd proven over and over again in school.

Granted, Mrs. O'Malley's rash was being stubborn. The unexplained low grade fever was also an issue. But Nicole was certain she would determine the reason.

"We've done a blood work-up. Blood chemistry has all come back normal. As well, the first culture did not turn up a viable reason for the breakout. At this point, I've ruled out viral causes and am in the process of ruling out bacterial infections."

"It sounds like you've been very thorough, Doctor."

Nicole beamed. "Diagnosis has been elusive so far, but I feel confident we'll find the cause and get the patient back on track medically."

Mrs. O'Malley drank some of the water she'd picked up shortly after Dr. Reed entered the room.

"Thirsty?" he asked the patient.

She looked at the cup in her hand as if surprised. "It's strange. I never used to like water. Now I find myself sipping at it all day long."

Nicole frowned. What did that have to do with a rash?

Damien turned back to her. "Have you tested her blood

sugar?"

Diabetes? He thought Mrs. O'Malley had *diabetes?* Nicole ran through the tests she'd ordered and the heat in her cheeks increased to inferno level. She wanted to crawl under the hospital bed and never come back out. No, she'd never tested the patient's blood sugar.

The medical encyclopedia in her head opened up to the page that dealt with complications of uncontrolled diabetes. Life threatening ones like coma and cellulitis were followed by lesser known symptoms. An unexplained rash was listed right there.

How could she have forgotten?

It took a real effort on her part to keep her hands from covering reddened cheeks. *Oh, God, her first week here and she'd already screwed up.* She shook her head. Well, there was nothing to do but own up to the colossal mistake she'd just made.

She glanced at her patient, who thankfully was busy watching Dr. Reed. "No, Doctor. I did not order a blood sugar. I'll be sure and order it stat."

"I think we'll have you fixed up in no time," he said to Mrs. O'Malley, patting her hand. What looked like a genuine smile on his face never wavered despite the fact he must be annoyed at the rookie mistake she'd just made. Even mortified as she was, she had to respect his ability to keep his emotions so well hidden.

"Can I speak to you outside, Dr. Milbourne?"

2

With her feet weighted by dread of the confrontation ahead of her, Nicole tried to hold her head high as she followed her boss out the door, certain she was about to be canned from the program.

Damien Reed put both hands in the pocket of his jeans and leaned back against the wall. The longer he stared across the corridor, the more Nicole began to sweat. This couldn't be good.

Well, better to confess up front than to wait and have it thrown in your face. "I'm sorry, Dr. Reed. I—I don't know why the possibility of a systemic disease like diabetes slipped my mind. I know better."

He closed his eyes. The look on his face was reminiscent of someone who'd just tasted heaven...or really great chocolate. When he opened them, she caught a quick flare of emotion before it disappeared behind his smile.

"Relax," he said. "Even if I thought you should be booted out of the program, I don't have the authority."

"Maybe not," she conceded. "But you have the ear of those who do."

He chuckled. "You've got me there." He pushed off the wall. "Walk with me."

She looked at the kit in her hand. "I really should get this to the lab."

Dr. Reed took it from her, pulled a pen from his pocket and, using the wall, wrote the patient's name and room number on it. Next, he waylaid a nurse. "Would you deliver this to the lab for me?"

"Certainly, Doctor." the nurse said. Twice his age, the woman glowed at the attention. Nicole rolled her eyes. The man had that affect on, well, just about everyone.

"Thank you," Nicole said to the nurse as she disappeared without any indication she'd heard Nicole's gratitude.

They walked in silence until he turned into a waiting room with nothing in it but a few chairs and neutral colors. Sitting, he motioned for her to take a chair across from him.

Here comes the boom. Nicole glanced at the picture above Dr. Reed's head. Did the sky over that sailboat indicate a storm was coming? Maybe. She settled her hands in her lap and waited.

"Why did you choose medicine for a career?"

The question came out of left field and Nicole felt her heart fill with the familiar ache of long ago memory. She clamped a lid on the pain and sat back, crossing her arms. "I don't see how that has any relevance to today."

"Humor me," he said. He leaned forward to rest elbows on knees, fingers laced together. "I'd like to understand your motivation."

"I have an interest in research," she finally answered. "Oncology research."

"That's on your resume. What I want to know is why?"

Nicole stared at green eyes that held both gentle question and firm resolve. She wasn't going to get out of answering. Over his head, the clouds in the picture seemed to darken. She didn't want to have this conversation, but he waited without moving until she finally answered.

"My mother passed away when I was ten years old."

"Cancer?"

She gave a quick nod. "Ovarian."

He cocked his head. "I'm sorry."

Nicole tried to shrug. She willed her shoulders to rise and show her indifference. Willed her head to remember that it had happened a long time ago. Willed her heart to stop thumping a painful reminder.

She should answer him. He was waiting, watching. After all these years, she still didn't know how to respond to that phrase. 'I'm sorry.' What the hell did that mean, anyhow? As she searched eyes filled with the patience of a man comfortable with silent pauses, she wanted, for the first time, to answer. "'I'm sorry' is such a strange phrase, don't you think? I'm not even sure I know what it means."

One dimple appeared. "It means something different for everyone. For me, it's all about what you went through, the pain you feel."

"Thank you." The unfamiliar sting of tears made her

blink and her fingernails dug into her hands as she tried to regain some control. "I'm sure, Doctor, that you didn't call me in here for a therapy session."

He studied her for a long moment before making some sort of decision. "No. I didn't. But it is nice to know you're capable of showing some emotion."

She straightened. "I beg your pardon?"

He held up a hand. "Don't get your bristles standing at attention. I meant no insult."

"Is there some point to this discussion, Doctor Reed? Am I in trouble?"

"For missing a lab test during your first week here? No. That's what I'm here to help catch. What I would like to offer you is some advice."

Relief threatened what little control she had over her emotions. She wasn't getting fired? Some part of her brain recognized the word "advice" but she couldn't get past the echo in her ears. She still had a job.

"—see the patient."

He was speaking. The man who'd just given her future back to her was speaking. She needed to listen. "Excuse me?"

"I said," he repeated as he stood. "Take time to get to know the patient. Don't just look at the body, or the symptom. Talk to the patient. Much of the time, the answers can be found in a simple conversation."

She stood and scuffed the carpet with her shoe. "That's the hardest thing for me," she admitted.

He smiled again and Nicole found herself drawn to the warmth. "It will get easier. Trust me. In the meantime, remind yourself to ask questions and listen to what they say. It's generally the best place to start when trying to diagnose an issue."

"Thank you, Doctor."

"I don't stand on formalities with my team. Please, call me Damien."

She shook her head. "You're my superior. And you've earned the title of doctor."

"So have you, Nicole."

"I know the diploma says that, but I don't believe it. Not yet."

"Trust me, in this program, you'll have plenty of opportunities to recognize how much you've earned the title." He glanced at his watch. "I've got other residents to check on. But I'll be watching...your progress with interest."

After he left, Nicole sank back down in the chair. The emotional upheaval of the last few minutes had wiped her out. She felt like she'd just finished a twenty-four hour shift. According to the clock, she still had eight of her twelve hours to go and, when the patient load ran heavy like today, shifts ran long. She'd learned that her first couple days in the program. Certain it was going to be a very long day and an even longer residency, Nicole headed back to work.

With a blood glucose meter in hand, she returned to Mrs. O'Malley's room. Taking Dr. Reed's advice, she spent some time talking to her patient. Listened would be more accurate, since the woman seemed to enjoy an audience and, given the opening, warmed to any subject.

That conversation told her, even before she tested Mrs. O'Malley, that her patient was diabetic. All the symptoms were there, and had been for some time. Her high blood sugar only confirmed it. It also explained why the rash was not improving. Nicole wrote up orders for further testing to confirm the diagnosis on paper, as well as insulin to bring her blood sugars down and regular blood sugar monitoring. She explained the diagnosis to the patient and rose to leave.

When Mrs. O'Malley began to fret, Nicole's instinct to run came back full force. Panic felt like a noose around her neck. Comforting patients was not something they taught in med school. She patted her patient's arm, trying Dr. Reed's technique, but the movement felt jerky and trite.

Plus, it didn't help. Mrs. O'Malley had started to sniffle and Nicole felt the noose tighten. She struggled to shrug it off and considered their conversation. The woman lived alone. She had a son, but he lived an hour away.

"You know," she said. "You won't go through this alone."

"But I don't have anyone to help me," she said, dotting at her eyes with a tissue from the box Nicole handed her.

"You've got a hospital full of people to help. You'll be well regulated on insulin before you leave here. You'll be taught how to take care of yourself, both with your insulin and your diet."

The worried frown on Mrs. O'Malley's face didn't budge much. In fact, the lines in her forehead deepened a fraction.

"Diet? You mean, I have to change the way I eat?" She latched onto Nicole's hand. "Does that mean no more lunches with my Red Hat Society? You *do* know what that is, don't you, dear? It's a wonderful group of women and oh, they are so dear to me. Do I really have to refrain from lunches? Oh, how will I ever learn all this?"

"It's all right, Mrs. O'Malley," Nicole said as she tried to extricate her hand from the woman's grip. "You'll still be able to eat with your friends. You will have to be a bit careful about the menu choices you select, but diabetes is a very functional disease."

Instead of being reassured, Mrs. O'Malley's grip tightened until it bordered on painful. "Oh, my. That's right. Diabetes *is* a disease. I have a disease. Me, who's been healthy all her life. How will I ever explain this to my son? And to my friends?"

Nicole took a deep breath and dug deep for the words that would reassure her patient. "Diabetes is very common, Mrs. O'Malley. In fact, I wouldn't be surprised to find out a few of your society friends had diabetes."

The woman paused and loosened her grip enough for Nicole to free her hand.

"Do you think so?"

"I know so." Nicole tried not to smile as Mrs. O'Malley smoothed her blanket, the picture of calmness now.

"And—" Nicole said. "We will have Home Health nurses come and visit you after your discharge until you're comfortable with everything. As well, I'm sure your son will involve himself as much as he's able to."

That did the trick. The last lines on Mrs. O'Malley's face relaxed.

Then, to Nicole's horror, tears started to trickle down her patient's cheek. Lord, what had she said now?

"Thank you," Mrs. O'Malley said. "Thank you *so* much."

Nicole nodded, the lump in her throat a wall her voice couldn't break through. She backed toward the door.

"You know, dear," Mrs. O'Malley continued. "I think you're going to be a fine doctor."

* * * * *

On her way home that night Nicole pulled her collar tight against an unseasonable September chill and reflected on the lesson learned today. A few minutes of conversation had not only helped with diagnosis, it had also completely mollified an agitated patient.

Spending time in a one-on-one conversation hadn't been easy, though. A shyness that bordered on painful had plagued Nicole for years. That was a significant part of why research appealed to her. She'd been first in her class in both undergraduate and graduate schools, but she knew her people skills were lacking. She also knew that today she had learned a very important lesson about being a doctor. And that it would be the hardest personal limitation for her to overcome.

Dr. Reed had gone easy on her. She was certain of it, even though she didn't understand why. She smiled at the memory of her name spoken in the rich timber of his voice, then forced the thought to the back of her mind. It wouldn't do to start fantasizing over the hunky head resident. She had too much to accomplish before she could even think about any sort of relationship. She chuckled, knowing that it was silly to even consider the possibility. No way would the inimitable Dr. Reed be interested in her.

Inside her apartment, Nicole dropped her bag and coat over a threadbare, but comfy-enough-to-fall-asleep-studying-on couch and walked the few feet to her tiny kitchen.

Small by just about anyone's standards, Nicole's apartment was a haven to her. After promising the landlord she would return the walls to the non-descript ivory most rentals required, Nicole had painted the kitchen a pale tangerine color that made her smile each time she walked into the room.

She started water heating for tea she hoped would revive her enough to do some research tonight. As tired as she was, she wouldn't be able to sleep until she determined how she had missed that diagnosis of diabetes today.

She would not make that kind of mistake again. The unwavering green eyes of Damien Reed came to mind and she wondered whom she was working so hard to impress.

3

"Good morning, Ms. Grant. I'm Dr. Reed."

Nicole side-stepped into the emergency room alcove as Dr. Reed greeted the patient. He may have said that initial mistake of hers meant nothing, but his actions over the past two months told a different tale. It felt like he'd materialized around each and every corner she turned, always pinning her with questions and firing away with another one almost before she finished answering the last.

That he'd selected her as his pet project was pretty much a given. Because of that, life had bordered on a living hell, with twelve to twenty-hour shifts followed by several hours of studying. Tea had been relegated to the back of her kitchen cupboard as coffee became her new best friend.

Nicole wasn't sure how much more of his attention she could take. And if the man asked her one more time what the patient had to say, she was going to scream. He'd sent her back into hospital rooms to *talk* time and time again.

Yep. Dr. Reed had it out for her. She shook her head, knowing that wasn't entirely accurate. He'd offered some very insightful comments and suggestions during their debates. The man was a gifted diagnostician on top of being good with people.

At odd times, she'd turn and find him staring at her, his face a strange study of intensity. It was as if he had more to say, yet wouldn't. Or couldn't. Damien Reed was a mystery. One which, at the moment, she didn't have the time or the energy to figure out.

From her spot near the privacy curtain, Nicole observed the petite woman who was the focal point of her orientation to her E.R. rotation. With a smattering of freckles across the bridge of her nose and translucent skin, Nicole placed her age at close to her own twenty-eight years. She squinted. Very close, as a matter of fact. The woman looked familiar. Her hair color was similar to Nicole's, although the woman's ran a bit more to the red than her own darker curls.

"Amanda?"

Dr. Reed and the patient both turned to her.

"Nikki? Nikki Milbourne?"

Damien Reed's eyebrows raised up and Nicole's cheeks warmed with color. "I go by Nicole now."

"Wow," Amanda said. "What's it been? Ten years?"

"Easily," Nicole answered. Since Damien stood there with quiet expectancy, she turned to him. "Mandy and I were roommates our first year in college."

"Those were good times," Amanda said, smiling.

Nicole remembered. Loaded down with studies, she'd begged off almost all of Amanda's invitations to go out and have a little fun. Almost. She glanced at Dr. Reed and found him watching her with undisguised amusement. *Great.* All she needed was for him to think she was some sort of party animal.

"Good times and a lot of work," Nicole said in an attempt to dispel any wrong impressions. "You left, what? Mid-Winter quarter, right? I never heard from you after that."

"Yeah. Sorry about that. My Mom got sick, so I went home to take care of her."

"She must have been pretty sick."

"She was. Breast cancer."

"I'm sorry."

"Me, too. We caught it too late. After a couple years of surgeries and chemotherapy, the cancer won."

Nicole gripped Amanda's hand. "I know what that's like."

Amanda nodded, her voice turning wistful. "Anyhow, after all that, college didn't seem so important anymore. I was working already, so I never bothered to go back." She smiled, the sparkle returning to her eyes. "But all that time you spent with your head buried in books paid off. You're a doctor, huh? Good for you."

"Thank you. I'm doing my residency here at Rochester Regional." She glanced at Dr. Reed, who watched her with a bemused concentration she couldn't categorize. One thing she did know. It was past time to get back on track. "Our relationship means I can't be your physician," She told

Amanda. She indicated Dr. Reed with her hand. "I'm confident Dr. Reed will take good care of you. And I'll stop by later to see how you're doing."

She turned to go, but Amanda held tight to her hand. "Please, stay." She worried her lower lip. "As my friend?"

Nicole hesitated, turning to Dr. Reed. He gave a quick nod of assent, so she moved around to the other side of the bed and stood silent as he began the process of diagnosing Amanda's pain. With his deep, mellow voice and quiet interest, he drew the information out.

Amanda Grant answered with confidence, even with the edge of worry Nicole could hear in her voice. She'd come to the emergency room with lower abdominal pain, primarily on the left side.

"How long have you had this pain, Ms. Grant?"

"Amanda will do just fine. Ms. Grant sounds like my career-minded maiden aunt." She smiled at Nicole. "No insult intended."

Nicole tucked her head as she stifled a grin.

"As for pain," Amanda said. "This time, it's been a day or so."

Nicole's head came up. "You've had this pain before?"

Dr. Reed glanced at her.

"Sorry to interrupt," she mumbled.

"A few times," Amanda answered. "It's been strange, kind of comes and goes." She grimaced. "Like now."

Dr. Reed continued. "On a scale of one to ten, how would you rate your pain at the moment?"

"About a five or six." The grunt as she finished the sentence validated her pain level. It took a few moments before she could continue. "It's been getting harder to ignore these last couple of months. I know I should have gone to my doctor, but work has been so crazy." She frowned and her hands settled across her abdomen. "This time, it's stronger than ever." She glanced at Nicole. "And it doesn't seem to be going away."

"What does the pain feel like?"

"It's like a deep ache. And low, off to the left."

Nicole felt a trickle of sweat begin to work its way down her spine as she fought to stay objective. Amanda's pain seemed localized, but it could still be one of many issues. It could be an inflammation in the colon, or kidney stones, or any number of things.

Or it could be ovarian pain. The thought sliced through her like a scalpel.

"Have you noticed any other issues?"

"Well, I've been more tired lately. That could be because I'm not eating all that well. Food just hasn't tasted that good."

Mental fingers in Nicole's brain went back to ticking off the illnesses that could account for these symptoms.

"I feel like I'm bloated. Then, yesterday I started to wonder if I had a bladder infection."

Hands curling into tight fists, Nicole fought for every ounce of strength she had to keep from backing up as dread tightened around her spinal column. She knew these symptoms. She turned wide eyes to Dr. Reed. At the imperceptible shake of his head, she forced her fingers to straighten and her hands to relax. She tried to focus on what Damien was saying but worry filled her ears with cotton.

Once he'd completed the physical examination and found tenderness in more than one spot, he turned to Nicole.

"What tests would you order, Doctor?"

Amanda grinned. "He's quizzing you, right?"

Nicole started to answer, but felt like she was chewing sand. Taking a moment to clear her throat, she recited a litany of tests she'd studied well over the course of her post-graduate studies.

"I'd order standard blood tests to check for an infection, as well as a—" Her voice broke and Amanda Grant's dimple disappeared.

"Sorry," Nicole muttered as another bead of sweat wound its way down her back. "Frog in my throat. I'd also order a...a CA-125, and a trans-vaginal ultrasound."

Dr. Reed nodded. "I concur." He turned to the patient. "We probably can't get some of these tests until tomorrow. I suggest we keep you in the hospital overnight."

"Oh, but I've got a meeting tomorrow that I have to be at."

Cancel it! Nicole wanted to scream the words, but she kept her lips tightly compressed.

"Can you bump it?" The casual warmth of Dr. Reed's tone was in direct opposition to the bile rising in Nicole's throat.

"Keeping you here means we'll get results faster," he said. "As well, we can do more to alleviate your pain in a hospital setting. Your pain was enough to bring you here, so it might be a good idea to give us some time to get it under control for you."

Back to worrying her lip, Amanda nodded her agreement.

Once out of the room, Nicole felt tears well up that were beyond her control. She started to shake. *Is it getting hot in here?* She tugged at the neckline of her shirt.

"I...need...some...air," she gasped.

Dr. Reed took her by the elbow and steered her out the emergency room doors, grabbing a blanket off the supply rack as he went by. Outside, he didn't stop until Nicole smelled the stale lingering scent of cigarettes. They were in the smoking shack? Thankfully, it was empty at the moment.

Nicole plopped into a chair. She knew Amanda Grant's symptoms and in fact, had studied them in depth. She gulped air in and felt a hand urge her head down between her legs as a blanket settled around her.

"Breathe, Nicole." His low tone soothed her, but not enough. She struggled to sit up.

Damien Reed wouldn't let her. Instead his hand moved across her back. The up and down motion, along with the sound of his voice saying words she'd didn't understand, eventually calmed her.

After several long moments, he allowed her up and snugged the blanket tighter around her shoulders. "Feeling better?"

"No." She shook her head. Curls that had escaped her bun settle around her face. "I mean yes, but no." She reached for his arm. "I know those symptoms. I *know* them because of my mother."

"It's too soon to know for sure."

"Everything adds up. All her symptoms point to an ovarian problem."

"Even if they do, it could be as simple as cystic ovaries. As a physician, you know better than to draw a conclusion before testing."

Nicole shot out of the chair and glared at him, the blanket falling to the cement. "Yes, I do. Except that I've studied this disease in depth. I know—"

His hand rose and, for a moment, Nicole thought he intended to touch her cheek. Then he dropped it to his side. "Don't make assumptions, Nicole. Wait for confirmation."

"I can't." The words came out on the end of a sob as she whirled on him. "Did you know what was wrong before you drew me in there?" She choked on the words. "Did you set me up for some sort of shock therapy?"

"I knew no more than you did. I think you know I wouldn't do that to you."

"It doesn't look good, does it?" Nicole whispered the words, afraid saying them out loud would make it real.

Damien picked up the blanket and settled it once again around her shoulders. "We won't know for sure until the tests come back."

He sank to a chair and massaged his temples. He was as affected by this as she was. She knew it, but overriding that realization was an almost paralyzing return to the day her mother had explained her own cancer.

Memories Nicole had struggled to bury for years resurfaced. She sat back down, tucking her hands underneath her. Too keyed up to remain that way, she hugged herself. Her breath frosted in the late November air and the ground sparkled with cold crystals. She didn't feel the chill. She was too overwhelmed by memories.

Damien's voice filtered through. "This isn't your mother, Nicole. It sounds tough, but you're going to see this situation a lot."

"I know that," she said. The words sounded hollow and far away.

His hand reached over to move a strand of hair out of her eyes. He stared at her hair as it curled around his fingers for a long moment before he pulled away. "This will sound harsh, but you need to decide if you can handle it."

Nicole jumped up and started to pace. "No." She shook her head, and then reached to pin her hair back into its usual bun. "I don't have to handle it. Or get used to it. I refuse to. This shouldn't have to happen. Not to her, not to my mother, not to anyone." She pounded her fists against her thighs. "*That's* why I've selected oncology research. So that the Amanda Grants of the world don't have to hear what you're most likely going to have to tell her in a couple days."

Damn it. She was so angry her body shook. And now she could feel the spilled tears on her face. Dr. Reed joined her. He tipped her head up and one thumb brushed at a wayward tear.

Nicole stared into eyes that showed compassion...and something else. She watched little lines deepen at the corners of those eyes as he smiled.

"I believe you will do just that, Nikki."

Damien Reed surprised the hell out of her then as he

pulled her into his arms. Only for a brief moment, then he released her and turned away, his deep intake of breath surprising her.

Nicole felt bereft. She wanted to stay in those warm, comforting arms. To be soothed by them. By him.

"Dr. Reed?" A nurse rounded the corner.

He stepped in front of Nicole, giving her time to get her tears under control.

"Yes?"

"We'll need orders to admit the patient in room six. And we've got victims en route from a multi-car accident. Dr. Jones asked if you could stay and help with triage."

Most people would miss the slump to his shoulders. Nicole noticed it, as well as the quick recovery. He wasn't untouched by the plight of the patients he treated. She wiped the last remaining dampness from her face. How much time would it take to develop a professional shell like his? *Too long*. She'd be well ensconced in a research facility long before she could grow the same hardened facade.

"Tell Dr. Jones I'll be right there," Dr. Reed said.

Once the nurse was gone, he turned back to Nicole. "I know patients like this are going to affect you."

"They affect you, too, don't they?"

He nodded. "They do. But I've had a little more time to figure out how to process it all."

"I can't imagine it ever being easy."

"Not easy, just easier to compartmentalize. You'll need to find a way to steel yourself no matter what the patient's issue is."

She sighed, knowing he was right.

He settled a hand on her shoulder. "I'll help you," he said. He took a few steps toward the E.R. doors and then turned back. "Get yourself together and join me for triage." His voice deepened. "And please, call me Damien."

She shook her head.

"I insist," he said with a grin as he disappeared.

Unable to get Amanda Grant off her mind, Nicole stopped in later that day. She found Amanda chewing away on her lower lip. "What's up?"

"Either this hospital works fast or you've got some pull around here, Doctor. The nurse just told me I'm going for that ultrasound test you ordered. They'll be here any minute."

Nicole chuckled. "Hospital time runs about the same as football time. It could be an hour or more." Hearing a commotion behind her, Nicole rolled her eyes. "They're here now, aren't they? Proving me wrong?"

Amanda leaned onto one elbow to see who or what was behind Nicole. With eyes no longer showing any trepidation, she nodded, a wide grin on her face.

A sense of satisfaction turned a bad day good for Nicole. She'd made Amanda forget, at least for a moment. On impulse, she offered to go with her to the test and Amanda's acceptance was quiet but heartfelt. When the procedure got a little uncomfortable and Amanda reached for her hand, Nicole tried to steel herself from the emotional double whammy. She cared about Amanda Grant. Add to that the realization that her mother had endured this same testing, and Nicole failed to find any sort of guard rail for her heart. Empathy wrapped its arms tightly around her and she couldn't honestly tell who was holding on tighter, she or Amanda.

4

At home that evening, Nicole took the salad she'd thrown together over to the table and sat down. It had been a long day and she was, once again, bone tired. With a sigh she looked at the pile of case histories she needed to review.

She picked at her lettuce, but wasn't hungry. Amanda Grant's situation overshadowed everything. Nicole was not well-versed in ultrasound images. At the moment, she was grateful for that lack of knowledge. She didn't want Amanda to see her recognize the worst case scenario. Hell, she didn't want Amanda to hear that scenario from her or anyone else.

She'd re-read the same paragraph three times when her phone rang.

"Hi, Nikki."

"Dad!" Her father must be psychic. How else did he

manage to call every time she needed a shoulder? "I'm glad you called." She tried to keep the quaver out of her voice.

"I thought I'd call and see how my best girl is doing. What's up?"

"Nothing. Everything's fine," she said.

"It doesn't sound like it. This is Dad you're talking to. Come on. Fess up."

He could always see through her attempts at being tough. "It's just been a long day."

"Long how?"

She sighed. He wasn't going to let her off the hook. She knew that. "I started my E.R. rotation today."

"You were looking forward to that, weren't you?"

"I was."

"Hmmmm. And now something has you not so enthused?"

"I had a tough patient to start out with."

"Tough how?"

Between hospital privacy laws and her knowledge that mentioning her mother would bother him, Nicole was unsure what to say.

"I let a patient get to me," she answered.

"Get to you? Get to you how? Did someone attack you, Nicole? Are you all right? Do I need to come out there?"

She laughed. Leave it to her father to misinterpret. The man's tendency to leap without thought was legendary. He'd explained one time how this issue, not an absence of love, had caused the demise of his marriage to her mother. "She wanted a security I wasn't able to give her," he'd said.

Nicole knew her step-mother had managed to settle

him down, and just in time, too, since her mother's death had led to a whirlwind courtship and wedding. Kate had taken over raising her and had done a good job. As good as she could.

Never able to have children herself, Kate had immersed their household in a revolving door of foster children. So much so that Nicole had always felt a bit like an outcast in her own home. She wasn't chosen. She'd come with her father as part of the package.

"Nicole? Are you all right?"

"Yes, Dad. Stop worrying. I didn't get attacked."

"Then what..." His voice, tinny through the phone, still made Nicole feel he was here in the room with her.

"I had a patient with some familiar, um, symptoms."

She could almost hear her father digesting the statement, searching for the positive spin. And then, unable to find it, coming to the right conclusion.

"Symptoms like what happened with your mother?"

"Yes." She whispered the word, wondering if she should knock on wood so as to not jinx Amanda Grant. She felt, deep inside, that no amount of woodwork could help her friend.

"And that hit you smack in the heart, didn't it?"

She pulled her feet up onto the kitchen chair, hugging her knees close enough to lay her cheek on, certain she could hear her heart pounding. "Yes."

She waited. Her father could always find the optimist's point of view. He could cheer her up when no one else could and he'd come through now, she was certain of it. He'd always come through in those clutch times. Which was why his next statement caught her so off guard.

"Honey, I know losing your Mom was tough. If this is too hard for you, maybe you should give it up. Come home and find a different line of work."

She jumped to her feet. "No. Absolutely not. I *want* to be a doctor. I have to. I *have to* find a cure."

"How are you going to get through this residency program? You're already mired in the same emotional empathy I saw in you as such a young child when your mother was sick." He sighed. "I know you. I know how hard you've guarded your heart since then. Almost to the point where you don't show emotions, period. If this patient is bringing all those feelings to the surface, what will the next patient do? I hate to say it, but this is going to happen again and again and again. You know that."

"Yes, I do know. It's funny that you say I guard my emotions. Damien says I need to toughen my skin. That it doesn't get easier, but it gets easier to deal with emotionally."

"Who's Damien?"

"Oh, sorry. I meant to say Dr. Reed."

"Isn't he that lead resident you've been complaining about since you started this program? How he's been picking on you and making you work harder than anyone else?"

"Yes. That's him."

"I see," her father said. "So, when did you get on a first name basis with someone who, up to this point, has seemed more like your nemesis?"

Nicole's mouth dropped open as she realized her

mistake. "He's, umm, still driving me hard." She tried to keep her tone neutral, in complete opposition to her flaming cheeks.

The laughter on the other end of the line indicated she hadn't pulled it off. *Damn*. "I didn't mean to call him Damien. And I don't. Not at work."

"You see him outside of work?"

"Never! He just...he asked me to call him Damien, all right?"

"Oh, really." He drew the word out in a way that teetered on very dangerous, very match-makerlike, territory. "This is starting to sound serious."0

Nicole's mind churned as she tried to find a way out of this conversation. Her father, a man to whom everything was funny, would not let this go. She gave it one last futile attempt.

"It's not like that. It's nothing but a working relationship. Even that will only last a few months. He's finishing up his final year of residency. That's why he's the lead."

"So he'll only be your boss a few more months, huh?"

Nicole could hear the laughter in his voice. "Drop it, Dad. I'm telling you, it's not like that. Not. At. All." Nicole suppressed the twinge of pain her words caused. Dr. Reed was the head of her team and nothing more. Really.

Then why do I keep remembering how good it felt to be in his arms?

"You know how much your mother and I would like you to find someone to share your life with," her father said.

32

Lord, could this conversation get any worse? "I know. But not right now. I need to focus on getting through this residency and settled into my research. There's plenty of time to meet someone after that. So, how's Kate doing?"

This time, he let her off the hook. "Oh, fine."

"Your tone doesn't sound fine to me."

"She's a little lost right now. No kids in the house, you know?"

Nicole chuckled. "Kate's always been happiest when she's chasing after children."

"Yes, she has. You know, she's your mother, too. It would be nice if you called her by that title."

Nicole straightened. They'd had this conversation before. "Has she said something?"

"No. And she never will," her father said.

Nicole felt the weight of her father's request once again settle on her shoulders. Her mother had died when she was ten years old. No one could replace her. "I'm sorry. I just...can't."

Her father was so quiet that she said his name again to make sure he was still there.

"I'm here. And I understand, even if I'm disappointed. *Kate* is actually the reason for my call. I think we need a change of pace."

Nicole frowned and looked outside her window. Even in the dark she could see light flakes signaling the season's first snow fall. "What kind of change?"

"Well, Kate's been sort of at loose ends. With no children in the house, and you on the other side of the country, I considered this might be a good opportunity for us to take a vacation. You know, get away from Seattle for a bit?"

Nicole sat up. "You're coming to visit? That would be great!" She looked around her tiny apartment and wondered how she'd fit them in, and then realized it didn't matter. They'd find room.

"Actually, I was thinking more along the lines of finding some warmer weather. I've booked us on a Caribbean cruise."

Somewhat deflated, Nicole got up and tossed her salad in the trash. "A cruise sounds like fun."

"I think it will be. I'm telling her about it tonight."

"I'm sure she'll love it."

"Here's the thing, Babydoll. We leave on Christmas Eve."

"Christmas Eve?" Her mind whirled. "But...I always come home for Christmas."

"I know. And I know how important that is to you. I think you know it's important to us, too."

Nicole's eyes stung with the effort to hold her emotions in check. Her chest felt like the weight of the world had just landed on top of it. Christmas was the one thing in her life that had never changed. Her mother had loved it. Her father and Kate had recognized that and made a big deal of the holiday.

"Here's the thing. Kate hasn't just been at loose ends. I'm worried she's depressed. She just sits all day and waits for the phone to ring...for another child to put her arms around. I think a change of pace might break her out of that melancholy."

She could very well believe that Kate was struggling. She knew what the kids meant to her. But to cancel Christmas? "I-I guess I understand."

"I knew you would. Thanks, honey. I know if I can get her to take the first step, she'll love the vacation."

Leaning against the counter, Nicole took a deep breath. "I'm sure she will. And I know the trip will be good for both of you."

"I think so, too. Now all I have to do is convince your mother."

"Good luck with that. I don't remember the last time you two went anywhere alone together."

"It's been a few years."

"Well, let me know how it goes when you tell her, okay?"

"I will. Thanks. I know this won't be the Christmas you're used to. But, you know, change can also mean opportunity. Maybe something will come up that will be even better than spending the holidays with us."

Nicole shook her head so hard curls hit her in the cheek. "Nothing beats Christmas at home."

"We'll see. In the meantime, you won't get away from us completely. We'll try to find a way to call you on Christmas Day. And I'm sure Kate will be mailing you a package."

Nicole hung up the phone, and then sat back down at the table. After several minutes of staring at blurry words, she gave up and headed for the couch and some mindless reality show on television.

Christmas. Her favorite day of the entire year. Her

mother had loved the season and decorated their house from top to bottom each year, even when she'd been so sick with cancer she could barely stand. She'd also always made sure Nicole's father shared in the celebration, something very few divorced couples could work out.

After...after her mother passed away, Kate had worked hard to make sure Christmas continued to be a special day for Nicole and for all of them.

Nicole had already spent Thanksgiving in the hospital cafeteria. With this change to Christmas, her entire holiday season was in an upheaval. This would be a first for her, not spending the holidays at home. And Nicole couldn't quite get past the worry that Christmas, for her, was forever changed.

5

Nicole wandered through hospital halls she probably knew better than her own apartment. She'd lost interest in the cheerful holiday decorations that adorned dull white walls and gleaming countertops, surrendering to the blurred dullness of too many long shifts. Another one of which she had just finished.

If she could make it to the intern's lounge without any more emergencies cropping up, Nicole could claim a few precious hours of sleep. She'd need them to get through her next twenty-hour rotation. Going home to her apartment was not an option due to time constraints and the December snowstorm that had dumped a foot of snow in the Rochester area.

Bone-tired now had meaning for her. It was all she could do to focus on putting one foot in front of the other.

"Ooomph!"

The stillness of night shift was broken by her collision with Brenda, one of the nurses.

"Sorry," Nicole said.

Nicole had shared some late night conversations with the nurse during rare quiet times. Primed for pre-med, Brenda had happily let pregnancy derail her. Nurturing was in her blood and the woman was good at it. Brenda eyed her now like a parent checking her child for injuries. "Are you all right?"

"Yes," Nicole said, hearing the weariness in her voice. "Just tired."

"Forgive me for saying this, but you look a little like death warmed over. You need some sleep, Doctor."

Nicole's head came up. Even after three months as a resident, she still wasn't used to the title of doctor. "I'm headed for sleep now." She glanced at her watch. Only five hours to her next rotation. "I hope I get enough to get through tomorrow. After that, I get an entire fourteen hours off." A weak smile was the only enthusiasm she could muster.

Brenda's smile showed her sympathy. "Get some sleep while you can," she said. She started to walk away, but turned back. "Hey, have you seen Dr. Reed?"

"Uh, not recently." *Thank goodness.* How could just the idea of Damien Reed make her feel so hyper-sensitive? It was like her skin remembered his touch. Nicole rubbed her arms as she asked Brenda why she needed Dr. Reed.

"His migraine patient is pretty miserable. I wondered if we could increase her pain meds."

Trying to shake the fuzz from her brain, Nicole asked

Brenda if there was anything she could do to help the patient.

"No, no. I'll page Dr. Reed. You," she said, wagging a finger at Nicole, "get some sleep while you can."

Nicole tossed a grateful wave in the air and dragged herself down the hall to the break room, praying it would be empty. No more conversations. She needed sleep.

The lights were low in the lounge, but she could see empty couches and she offered a quick prayer of thanks. Grabbing a pillow and blanket off the pile pilfered from various linen carts, she took a grateful step toward one of the couches.

The scrape of a chair turned her in the opposite direction, where the illumination from a small desk lamp verified she wasn't, in fact, alone.

Dr. Damien Reed sat hunched over a book. Nicole craned her neck to see what he was reading. It looked like a medical manual. He didn't even twitch an ear at her arrival which was unusual.

Over the past few weeks, he'd been everywhere. Each time she turned a corner, ordered a lab test, or evaluated a new patient, he was either involved or nearby. That presence should have calmed her. Instead, she found it difficult to focus. She learned firsthand that his reputation for patient advocacy was fairly earned. Even more than that, he cared about his patients. She respected him for that. And told herself for the hundredth time that is was his professionalism she was drawn to.

His shaggy hair was more unkempt than usual. It stood out at angles in strange spots, as if he'd been running his hands through it and stopped midway. He'd taken his lab coat off. It sat crumpled on the chair next to the desk.

Muscles rippled across his back as he turned a page. How did the man stay in such good shape when he spent almost every waking minute here at the hospital? She barely remembered to eat, let alone exercise.

Damien hung his head. The sigh he emitted echoed through the room, sending vibrations of compassion through Nicole. She glanced longingly at the bedding she held, and then tossed it aside and poured two cups of coffee.

Nicole tried to set the cup on the desk with care. She really tried. What she hadn't factored in was his complete focus on the textbook in front of him. The cup hit the desk for all of two seconds and then went airborne in response to his reflexive startle. The coffee stain spread down her lab coat in mocha-colored fingers. Nicole stared down at it, then up into the shocked face of Damien Reed.

"I'm sorry," he said.

She pulled the soggy jacket off, wadded it up, and tossed it into a nearby laundry bin. "Lab coats are a dime a dozen. It's my fault. I shouldn't have surprised you."

His only response was a quick nod as he turned back to the textbook.

"What? No retort?"

Damien didn't answer and that's when Nicole started to worry. She pulled his lab coat from the chair and sat down. As she settled the jacket on her lap, she smelled something all male. It wasn't cologne. They weren't allowed to wear it due to allergy issues. It was Damien Reed's scent, warm spice with a touch of hospital antiseptic thrown in, and it drew her in. Nicole clenched her jaw against the desire to bury her face in the coat.

When she looked up, she could see his eyes almost as unfocused as hers and as red as a student in a No-Doze cram session for finals. She knew the look and most likely mirrored it, except with him, deep worry lines around his eyes and mouth enhanced the weariness.

"Are you all right?"

He scrubbed his face with his hands. "I'm fine. It's my patient I'm worried about."

Nicole knew about worry. This residency seemed to have broken through that self-imposed emotion-guard her father had mentioned. She'd worried and fretted over too many patients these past few months and she wasn't sure she could handle the repetitive ache of concern.

In an attempt to lighten Damien's mood, she asked him what happened to compartmentalizing work.

His answering scowl proved how truly concerned he was.

"What's up?"

"I try not to worry. Most of the time, it works. This one's tough. I hate to see people in pain."

"End-stage situation?"

"I don't know." He rubbed his chin. "God, I hope not."

Nicole reached out to comfort him, but pulled back unsure of how that would be received. She wanted to smooth the lines from his forehead and see again the smile she'd become accustomed to. Instead, she clutched his lab coat in her hands. Sentiment, however well-meaning, would not help him solve his patient's dilemma.

Leaning an arm on the desk, she quizzed him. "What symptoms does the patient present with?"

The ghost of that smile she wanted to see returned as he straightened. "So the lead resident now becomes the student?" he asked.

She arched an eyebrow in response and it took only a moment before he grabbed the bait.

"All right, Doctor. A twenty-two year old female arrived about twelve hours ago with debilitating head pain, photosensitivity, and extreme emotional distress."

"Did you *talk* to the patient?"

This time, he did break out in a smile. "In depth."

"Social history?"

"Mother and father are still alive. Two siblings. No family history I can relate to this."

Nicole nodded. "Has she had anything like this before?"

"No."

"What's going on in her life right now?"

"The family's not well off. She entered college early and has been funded almost completely by scholarships and grants. She also finished early and is cramming for her GRE exam for graduate school."

"Could this be stress related?"

"Possibly." He cocked his head. "We can't rule that out."

"Migraine?"

"It appears so, except the standard medication regimen isn't doing much to alleviate her pain."

"Have you done a spinal tap?"

Damien nodded. "Yes. In fact, I was pinning my hopes on meningitis being the issue, but the test was negative."

Nicole was at a loss. "That about takes care of any possibilities I can think of without doing more research."

The buzz of Damien's pager sounded harsh in the quiet room.

"That about your patient?"

"Yes." Damien pushed off the desk and stood.

Nicole stood with him, handing him the now wrinkled lab coat. "Maybe talking to her again would give you more clues?"

"I agree," he said. "But I need to get her pain under control first."

"Would you like me to go with you?"

One side of his mouth quirked up. He reached to brush a strand of hair back from her face and traced a tender line down her cheek. "No. However I look, you look worse."

"Thanks," she said with a laugh that vanished under the intensity of his gaze. Tough patients, sleep deprivation, everything negative in her life at the moment faded as she let her eyes show what her words could not. She cared for Damien Reed much more than she should.

She no longer felt tired. In fact, she wanted this moment to go on forever. His hand cupped her chin. Her eyes dipped to his lips. She'd let his smile lull her to sleep more nights that she could recall. Now, desire overrode sense. She wanted to feel those lips on hers.

He lowered his head one agonizing centimeter at a time. Nicole's breath was nothing but infinitesimal puffs of air as she waited for the touch she'd dreamed about.

The door behind them creaked open and another resident stepped in. "Oh," he said. "Sorry."

Nicole never did figure out how Damien managed to put distance between them so fast. "No need to be sorry," he told the doctor. He stared at Nicole for a long moment before motioning to the couch. "Get some shut-eye." Without another word, he strode out of the room.

Nicole stared at the door long after it closed behind Damien. Her hand went to the lips he had almost touched. *What had just happened?* Always gentle, he was hands-on with his patients, but maintained a hands-off policy with the residents. The frustrated rumor-mill was proof of that.

When she noticed the resident watching her, she grabbed the bedding from the floor and headed for a couch. Damien could have any woman in the hospital if he wanted. On more occasions than she could count, she'd overhead invitations. For dinner, for drinks, even suggestions of more intimate gatherings. Nicole frowned.

Why would he almost kiss her? And, why, oh why hadn't he been faster at it.

She scowled at the interrupting resident, and then settled back into the pillow to let dreams of a dark-haired physician carry her off to sleep.

The jarring pager vibration, her wakeup call, brought Nicole around to a groggy reality. She blinked her eyes several times, trying to dispel the fog that saturated her vision. She recognized the break room and sat up, rubbing her eyes to help them stay open.

It didn't work. A glance at her watch explained why.

She'd gotten a mere three hours of sleep. Nicole leaned against the couch back, running fingers through her hair and wondering how she was ever going to survive in this sleep-deprived state.

Standing to stretch still tired muscles, Nicole sniffed. The odor of burnt coffee permeated the air. *Great.* Someone left an empty pot on a hot burner...again.

After cleaning the pot and starting a new one, she went down the hall to freshen up. Glancing in the mirror, she was dismayed at the circles under her eyes. Not black, but certainly an early charcoal. She pulled at the skin on her cheek. Was it losing its elasticity? When was the last time she'd been outside or seen sunshine?

With coffee in hand, Nicole decided to check on Dr. Reed's patient before starting her own shift. She stepped into the darkened room and found him slumped over in a chair on the far side of the hospital bed, asleep.

"He's been like that for an hour or so now."

The whisper came from the bed and Nicole turned to the patient. She wasn't much younger than Nicole, but frailty stole years. She appeared petite, and maybe a little underweight. Her brown hair hung limp. Her eyes were open, and even in the darkness, Nicole could tell they were a startling lavender color.

Nicole smiled. Her voice barely above a whisper, she cocked her head toward the man in the chair. "So I caught the boss sleeping on the job, eh?"

The girl let out a soft chuckle, but even that effort creased her brow.

Nicole held out her hand. "I'm Dr. Milbourne, one of

the residents here."

"Mary Smith," she said, giving Nicole's hand a feeble shake.

"Pain still bad?"

"It's...a little better."

"But not much," Nicole said.

"No." She tried to shake her head, but the grimace on her face said even that was too much movement.

"Don't try to move. I just stopped by to see if I could help." She motioned to the chair. "I see you're in good hands."

"I...just wish this pain would go away." Tears welled up in the lilac eyes.

"If anyone can find out what the problem is, it's Dr. Reed," Nicole said. It wasn't much, but she felt the need to offer the girl hope.

"Thank you for that vote of confidence, Dr. Milbourne."

Nicole's head shot up as Damien Reed straightened. He had a clearly defined five o'clock shadow. Nicole had never been attracted to beards, but on him, it looked good. Too good. The vision of that cheek up against hers warmed her own face to the point where she was glad the lights were low.

Keeping her voice quiet, she asked if there was anything she could do to help.

"Not unless you've got a suggestion for pain reduction," he said as he rubbed sleep out of his face.

"I'd be up for that," Mary said.

Nicole smiled at the patient. "I've seen how hard Dr.

Reed's working to reduce your pain level."

"I know he is. And it's worked—a little," she said.

"But not enough," Damien finished, his lips thin lines. "I've ordered a CT scan."

Nicole nodded, knowing a scan would be to rule out bleeding issues. Checking her watch, she realized she was just about overdue for rounds. "I've got to go, but if there's anything I can do to help, page me."

"Thank you," Damien said. His eyes mirrored the gratitude in his voice and Nicole carried that memory with her through another long day of patient care.

6

Nicole set her tray on a cafeteria table and slumped down into a chair. It was way too late to be eating dinner, but she needed something in her stomach. She took a bite of mashed potato, grimaced, and set her fork down. How could her stomach growl even as her throat closed up, unwilling to swallow?

It had been the day from hell. She'd picked the worst day to be late for rounds. Dr. Jones, the attending physician who oversaw the entire residency program had chosen today to pop in and supervise the residents. She'd heard he did this to the first-year students as a way to catch them off guard and wean the ones who couldn't take the pressure.

Not a good day to show up late. He'd noted her entrance with nothing more than a glance. He then proceeded to chose her for the worst and most menial tasks for the remainder of the day. Nicole had worn a path in the linoleum going back and forth to the lab. He'd asked her for initial impressions with each new case. At least she'd held her own in that respect. So far, she was five for five on her diagnoses being correct.

Then she'd gone in to treat little Riley Macon. Nicole palmed her forehead in frustration. A simple fracture, Dr. Jones had said. But Nicole had observed much more while casting the boy. Eight years old, he appeared more like a six year old. His hunched stature, like the mother who would not let go of his hand, didn't feel right. The father stood in the corner with his arms crossed and no one said a word except to answer a question. Their answers were monotoned and monosyllabic.

"Yes, Doctor."

"No, Doctor."

That was all she could get out of them. When she'd tried to help the boy take his shirt off, he'd clutched it to his body. Not, however, before she'd caught a glimpse of a dark bruise. Knowing something wasn't right, she'd muttered something about needing additional supplies and searched out the attending, who, with multiple victims en route from an accident, had been very clear about his lack of interest in her concerns.

"Discharge him now, Dr. Milbourne. Let his primary care physician handle it. We need the room for more serious cases."

Instead, Nicole had pulled up hospital records showing three visits in the last six months, all for unrelated injuries. Then she'd called social services, who called child protective services.

The father had been removed from the room against his will. It had taken several guards to subdue him and he was now in police custody. Nicole stood in the back of the room as the mother and boy revealed, word by slow word, a long history of mental and physical abuse.

They'd get the help they needed now.

Deepened lines on Dr. Jones' face illustrated his annoyance with her as he overheard her being congratulated for seeing the true issue. She'd pay for going over his head. That much was certain.

"Rough day?"

Nicole looked up to see Damien standing there with a tray. She waved to the other seat at her table and he joined her.

"Let's see." She started ticking off reasons on her fingers. "I was late for rounds, so your boss used me as his personal sounding board and errand girl. Then I went against his orders on a case, so I'm guessing my life is going to change from an exhausted purgatory to a living hell for a while."

He chuckled. "I heard what you did for that boy and his mother."

How could he have heard?

"It may be a large hospital, but the really juicy stories get around quick. And shaming the man most nurses love to hate is definitely news that moves." He chewed a bite of his sandwich before speaking again. "You did the right thing, you know."

Nicole nodded. She knew. Hearing him say it made her feel better. She picked up her fork and started in on her salad.

They ate in companionable silence until her cell phone rang. Damien made a move to leave, but Nicole waved him to stay. "It's my Dad. I'm sure it won't take long."

"Hi, Nikki," Kate said.

So it wasn't her Dad. "Hi, Kate. How's everything going?"

"As well as can be expected. Honey, your father told me about the cruise he booked."

The trip that had changed everything about Nicole's holiday. She tried to stifle the resentment, but it wasn't easy. "You should have fun," she said.

"I told him I couldn't agree without talking to you, dear. I know how much the holidays mean to you. We won't go on this cruise without your blessing."

Nicole felt the power shift to her. She felt Kate's honest need for her consent. And she felt like a heel for her role in Kate's needing that approval.

It appeared she would be spending her first Christmas alone. She glanced at Damien, but he appeared more interested in finding a way through the saran wrap that encased a chocolate chip cookie than in her conversation.

She closed her eyes. *Buck up, Nicole. It's only one holiday*. She tried. She tried really hard, but the quaver in her voice didn't quite disappear. "Go. Have fun. You've more than earned this." She smiled, hoping the action would infuse her voice with cheerfulness. "Fun is good for the spirit, you know. I'm a doctor. I should know."

"But you'll be alone for Christmas," Kate said.

Ouch. The stark realization hurt, but she again snuffed

the seed of resentment as much as she could. "It's only one holiday, right? We've had a lot of them and we'll have a lot more. I'm thrilled for both of you, getting away for this first time ever on a vacation by yourselves. Honest."

"Thank you, dear. I know this must not be easy for you. You know we'll miss you, don't you?"

She tried not to choke up. "I'll—I'll miss you, too."

"We'll call you as close to Christmas as we can, but it will depend on where we're at and if we have reception. We love you."

"I love you, too. Talk to you soon, Kate."

Nicole flipped her cell closed and tucked it away in her lab coat. She pushed her salad away and stared out the window.

"Folks going away for the holidays?"

"Yes."

"Where to?"

"A cruise along the Mexican Riviera."

"And you're not happy about that."

She straightened. "Of course I'm happy for them. Why wouldn't I be? They not only raised me, they joined the foster parent program and have helped a lot of kids find solid ground. Kate, especially, is selflessly devoted to helping children. She also took me on shortly after meeting my dad. And now, finally, they're getting away on a vacation that's just the two of them."

Damien nodded. "Why do you call her Kate instead of mother?"

He bit into his cookie as Nicole turned back to stare outside, ignoring the subject she knew he wasn't done with.

He proved her right after he finished eating. "You're upset they are leaving over the Christmas holiday."

She turned to him tight-lipped, but the simple truth stole her resolve. Nicole felt her lip quiver. "It's always been an important holiday for us to share as a family. My mother," her voice broke a little further, "loved Christmas. Dad and Kate always made sure it was a special day for me."

"So now it's time for you to create your own kind of special Christmas."

Nicole stood and slapped her half-full plate on the tray. The man was good at driving the obvious home. "Yes, Doctor. Now I get to figure out how to enjoy a holiday I love while being buried beneath an overwhelming work load and crazy hours."

She stalked off, not caring one whit what he thought. Nicole didn't get far before a hand on her arm stopped her.

"I'm sorry. My intention was not to anger you."

But you did. She stared at him for a long moment, then relented, feeling her shoulders relax as the anger drained away. "I know you didn't. I'm being way too sensitive...and selfish."

He crooked his arm and smiled. "Come on. Sit with me while I finish my coffee."

It was hard not to get pulled into those eyes, especially when they crinkled up at the edges like now. Nicole bit back a smile, but it took a tremendous effort. "All right."

He refilled her coffee cup and settled down across from her.

"How's your patient, Mary, doing?" Nicole figured patient care would be a safe topic.

"Pain's slowly diminishing, but we've got her on some pretty heavy meds to make that happen."

"Any results from the CT scan?"

"Preliminary only," he answered. "There's no indication so far of any bleeding issues, arteritis, or aneurysm."

"That's good," Nicole said with a nod.

"Very good," Damien agreed. "Except we still don't know what's causing all this. To top it all off, she's got a low grade fever now and some migratory joint pain."

Nicole frowned. "These are new symptoms?"

"Yes." Damien ran both hands through his hair and Nicole couldn't help but notice how easily he did that. She wanted to run her own hands through the wavy dark lengths. Mentally shaking herself, she focused on what he was saying.

"—not used to this. I'm a good diagnostician."

"You are," she said.

He slapped a hand on the table, their coffee slopping over the edges of the cups. "Yet I can't figure out what's wrong with this patient. I can't ease her pain."

Nicole reached out and covered his hand with hers. "You *will* figure this out. I'm certain of it."

He covered hers with his free one and they both stared at their hands, before Nicole reluctantly pulled hers away. "Have any other symptoms exhibited themselves?"

"She had what appeared to be a bout of confusion this afternoon. The migraine could explain that."

"Chronic fatigue syndrome?"

"I considered that, but it doesn't account for the

54

photosensitivity. Plus, she jogs regularly and has no trouble recovering from that."

"Depression?"

"It doesn't fit the pattern. I've also considered eating disorders. And I've ruled out thyroid issues."

She wracked her brain for something that would encompass the wide ranging symptoms. "Fibromyalgia?"

He crooked his head. "Maybe."

Just then his pager went off. He glanced at it and jumped up. "It's Mary."

Nicole followed, barely keeping pace as he launched himself up the stairs two at a time. By the time she reached the fourth floor, she was out of breath and he was no where to be found. She hurried to his patient's room and found it alive with activity.

Without turning, he spoke to Nicole. "She's seizing."

She knew all they could do was help her ride it out. It took a while, but Mary's body eventually settled into an exhausted, almost comatose state.

After everyone else emptied out of the room, Damien pulled a chair close to the bed. Nicole, now off the clock, contemplated the fourteen hour reprieve she was due for. Her own bed, in an apartment she hadn't seen for several days, beckoned.

As she watched the physician she'd come to greatly admire, she knew she wouldn't be going home anytime soon. "I'll be back in a moment," she told him.

He never looked up or even acknowledged her comment.

Nicole raced to her locker and grabbed her textbook of diseases. Taking it back to the patient's room with her, she pulled a chair next to Damien's and opened the book.

It took some time to find it, but the thread of symptoms eventually led her to a possibility. "Damien?"

He must have caught the excitement in her voice because he straightened and leaned toward her. "Have you found something?"

"I think so. Although there's no telltale rash."

He stared at her.

"Damien, I think she has an auto-immune disorder. I think she has Lupus."

He remained mute, but she saw the spark of belief flare in his eyes. He glanced at the patient and then back at Nicole. "I think you've hit on it." His voice was a rushed whisper as he reached for the textbook and read. "It's all here. Joint pain, headache, even the seizure can be tied to this diagnosis."

He stood, handing her the book. "I've got to order some additional tests. And some steroids to help ease her symptoms." He strode toward the door, but quickly returned to Nicole's side, pulling her up and into his arms. "Doctor, you have earned your degree today." He gave her a quick kiss on the lips, then was out the door before she could react.

Nicole sank to the chair, her fingers gliding over lips that still felt the imprint of his. She hugged her chest, trying to hold close the warm tingle from their embrace. A slow smile spread across her face. Today was a good day.

She glanced at her watch. Tonight, actually. It was after

2A.M. and she was overdue for some sleep. As she watched the patient's chest rise and fall in measured breaths, Nicole settled into a comfortable position in the chair and wait for Damien's return.

There was really no other place she wanted to be right now than by his side.

7

A gentle caress filtered through the mud of deep sleep and got Nicole's attention. She curled into it, not yet ready to wake up. It grew more insistent. She brushed the touch away, but it returned.

Opening one eye, she pinpointed the irritation as Damien's grinning face came into view. She groaned as she opened up both eyes and tried to figure out where she was. This wasn't her bedroom. It was a hospital room.

It hit her as she stretched. She was still in Mary's room. Damien's patient. She looked around. The room was awash in daylight, something that had been intolerable for Mary. Yet here she was, awake, sitting up in bed, and smiling.

Nicole's lips quirked up. "You feel better," she said.

"Yes, I do," Mary said. "Not perfect, but the headache is down to a dull roar."

"We've still got a ways to go to get the inflammation

down," Dr. Reed said to Mary. "But you've responded quickly and well to the initial medications. You'll need to continue under the care of a rheumatologist, but I think it's safe to say you'll be able to go home in a day or two."

"I like that idea. The best news of all is that I spoke to the head of the department my studies are in," Mary said. "I think they'll grant me a time waiver so I can still take my exams."

Nicole's grin widened. "That's great news." She stretched again, trying to ease muscles stiffened by sleeping in a chair. "How long have I been asleep?"

"About four hours," Damien said. "I didn't have the heart to wake you."

Her watch verified the time. "Well," she said, "I've still got about ten hours left before I'm back on shift. I think I'm going home to shower and change clothes." She looked down at the wrinkled khakis she'd been wearing for somewhere around thirty six hours. "These are definitely past their prime."

Damien walked her out. In the hall, he took both her hands in his. "Thank you for finding this solution. I don't know why I didn't see it."

"You would have gotten there. I didn't put the symptoms together for a long time, either. Lupus is tough to diagnose."

He nodded. "I—" He shuffled from foot to foot. When an orderly passed by them, Damien dropped her hands and stuffed his deep into his pockets. "I hope you get some more rest. You've certainly earned it."

She frowned, wondering what he had really meant to

say. "I'll settle for a chance to do some laundry and eat something that's not hospital food."

Damien laughed. "I know what you mean. I can't remember the last time I had a home cooked meal."

"Well, I'm not a gourmet chef, but I know my way around a kitchen. We could celebrate with a home cooked breakfast at my place." Nicole felt the breath whoosh out of her lungs and struggled to keep from clamping a hand over her mouth. She knew she was as red as the blood rushing to her face. Had she really invited her boss, the hunky Dr. Damien Reed, over for an intimate meal for two?

"Um, I mean, um, well, I'm sorry. That was forward of me. You're my boss, after all. Forget I said that, okay?"

She would have turned and run, but he stopped her with three simple words.

"I'd love to."

She gulped, thinking of the current state of her apartment, the fact that she now needed to pick up groceries, and that she only had a few short hours to get through all this and be on shift here at the hospital. "All right."

"When and where?"

Damien's voice had dropped into the deep, quiet range she found sexy as hell and Nicole felt her hormones answer. It was going to be a long morning.

She wrote down her address for him, picked an hour that hopefully would give her enough prep time and get her back to work by her shift. As she left the hospital, she realized snow had begun to fall again in earnest. It was a good thing both the twenty-four hour grocery store and her apartment were within walking distance. She was a lousy snow driver.

A rushed three hours later her apartment had some semblance of order to it, a breakfast casserole baked away in the oven, and the smell of home made bread filled the room. Brewing coffee dripped away and dishes were in place on the table.

Nicole stood in front of her small closet wondering what on earth she should wear for breakfast with her boss.

Her boss.

She said the words over and over again. Somewhere, over the past few days, she'd stopped thinking of him that way and that was dangerous. She didn't have time for relationships, most certainly not a complicated one that broke rules she had agreed to when entering this program. Not that it was even a possibility. There was no way Damien Reed thought of her in that way.

Nicole turned this way and that in the mirror, wondering how he saw her. Granted, she was trim, but her breasts were too small and her legs too long. She yanked a dark green turtleneck over her head, and slipped into a wool skirt. She simply did not have any "date" clothes.

As she ran a brush through her hair, she frowned, wishing she had a more vibrant hair color than mousy brown with a touch of red. Maybe when she finished her residency and actually earned a living wage, she'd have it foiled and add some blond highlights. She started to pin it up, but decided against it and let the soft curls settle around her shoulders. At least she was lucky enough to have her mother's thick hair. Getting it under control for work took some doing.

How many years had it been since someone had brushed her hair? Her mother used to style and braid it often. She'd loved those times. They had talked about everything. In her stepmother's defense, Kate had tried. Nicole remembered how much of a brat she'd been about Kate doing her hair and felt a twinge of guilt. She'd been pretty hard on her stepmother and wondered how Kate had managed to tolerate it.

Nicole was startled out of her reverie by the doorbell. She hadn't put a lick of makeup on but was officially out of time. Damien would have to take what he got.

She glanced through the peephole, a conditioned response, and her eyes widened as she saw him straightening his tie. The man didn't wear a tie at the hospital, but he wears one to breakfast with...a co-worker?

She glanced down again at her drab skirt. A debutante, she wasn't. *Oh, well.* She opened the door.

Damien picked something up from the floor and straightened. A plant. He had brought a plant? Nicole felt more confused than ever. "Hi," she said.

"Hi." He held out the poinsettia. "I brought this as a thank you."

She took it from him, hugging the pot to her chest, knowing the apartment behind her showed no holiday spirit. In fact, it looked pretty much the same as it had every other day.

"Thank you," she said, burying her face in petals she knew had no real scent. "It's very thoughtful of you."

He pulled his hand around from behind his back. "I,

um, also brought this."

The bottle wasn't wine. It was maple syrup and in one of the New England states signature leaf-shaped jars. She stifled a grin, knowing she had a jar exactly like it in her closet, ready to ship to her folks for the holidays.

He cocked his head, smiling. "It's a little too touristy, isn't it?"

"It's perfect and I love it. Thank you." She motioned him in.

"I was going to bring wine as a gift, but since this is a breakfast..." The words trailed off as he set the syrup down and shrugged off his coat.

She laughed. "Wine would be good if I have to spend another day under Dr. Jones' thumb."

"Is he still giving you trouble?"

"No more than you do." Nicole's hand flew to her mouth when she realized what she'd said. "Sorry," she mumbled.

"It's just part of the service we offer as mentors, I guess," he said, laughing.

Nicole decided then and there that if making her life difficult made him laugh like this, it was worth it.

"Flaying the backs of your interns is *not* funny," she said. Her efforts at being serious failed as the corners of her mouth tugged upward.

She settled the poinsettia on the end table, turning it this way and that. He laid his coat over the arm of the couch and watched until she had it just right. With a final tap on one of the leaves, she picked up the syrup and turned back to Damien.

"You know, I could talk to Dr. Jones if you like," Damien said.

"Who's going to talk to you?"

He raised his eyebrows. "Have I really been that hard on you?"

"Yes," she shot back. "You have." She sighed, knowing that wasn't the truth. "I'll admit I think it's made me a better doctor. Thank you for that."

Damien inclined his head in acknowledgement. "So you don't want me to talk to him?"

"No." She was vehement. "He's got it in for me at the moment, but I can take care of my own problems."

"I like that about you," he said, his voice low.

Nicole felt the heat of a blush tinge her cheeks and turned away to hide it. "Breakfast is almost ready," she said.

He followed her into the kitchen which, for the first time since she moved in, felt claustrophobic.

"I like this," he said.

She looked around at the small, tangerine-colored room. "That's the idea. I needed a cheerful place."

He sniffed. "And it smells great, too."

"You may want to reserve judgment on that until you taste it." She pulled the casserole out and set it on the table.

Damien leaned over her shoulder. "It looks as good as it smells."

She nodded, unable to speak with him so close. Did it seem like he stayed there longer than was necessary? He backed away and Nicole decided it must have been her imagination. She cleared her throat. "Warm food seemed like a good choice, considering the weather."

Damien pulled back the curtain and Nicole glanced outside. Snow fell in big, white flakes. It probably wouldn't stop for hours, but this was New York. Snow didn't stop life here. It didn't even slow it down.

She set the syrup on the table. "I didn't make anything this can go with."

"It's a gift. Use it when you need to. Of course," he paused, "if it meant an invitation for another home cooked breakfast, I wouldn't be opposed."

"Ah, so you have a plan," she said, slicing the bread.

"I do have a plan," he said.

Nicole paused at the focus she heard in his voice. She didn't get the chance to question him, though, as he changed the subject.

"I didn't notice any holiday decorations."

"That's not true. There's a lovely poinsettia sitting front and center in my living room."

"But nothing else?"

"There's been no time to decorate," she said. *Translation: I spend my meager salary on food and rent instead of decorations.*

Still, the pang of a Christmas without them hit hard and Nicole sighed. Shaking her head, she set bread slices out and served up sections of the egg, potato, and sausage casserole. They sat down at the two-person table she'd nabbed from a graduating student last summer. It had always worked fine for her. Now, the area felt small and confining. Somehow, being close enough to touch knees with Damien Reed did strange things to her nervous system.

"The casserole's hot. Be careful."

He forked a bite, and then leaned in to blow gently on it. Nicole felt a tingle weave its way through her body and settle somewhere low in her stomach as she watched. His eyes met hers and he winked before popping the forkful in his mouth.

Then his eyes widened in pleasure. "This is good. Very good, in fact," he said. The look on his face said he hadn't expected that.

"Thanks for the vote of confidence." Nicole laughed.

At least he had enough humility to look sheepish. She cocked her head. The look was kind of endearing on him.

He paused mid-bite. "What?"

"Nothing," she said, focusing on her own plate.

"You had a funny look on your face," he said, grinning.

She didn't know how to answer. She'd never been one to hedge, but this...attraction was new territory for her. She opted for a piece of the truth. "I guess I'm just not used to seeing you away from the hospital."

"I like you this way." She stared at the napkin she had started to shred, wondering what cupboard she could crawl into.

The fact that Damien didn't laugh scared her more than just about anything. Instead, he covered her hand with his. "I like this, too."

Breakfast forgotten, she stared at their hands as unfamiliar warmth washed through her body and settled like a comforting blanket around her. She tried to stop her heart from overriding her mind.

When she looked up, darkened green eyes stared back

at her and she knew everything she'd tried to convince herself of wasn't true. He felt it, too. She could see it reflected in those eyes.

When he leaned forward, her heart began to pound against the inside of her chest. *He's going to kiss me.*

He paused a fraction of a second from her lips. She sensed no indecision. Maybe he, like her, wanted to savor this moment. To feel it unfold like a slow ripple in time.

When their lips touched, that ripple expanded until there was nothing in her world except Damien and the paradise she felt as they kissed.

This was no hot and bothered I-need-sex-now kiss. Instead, there was a sweetness, a gentle discovery to it that wove a cocoon of emotion around her heart.

When he pulled away, she could have sworn she heard a softly whispered "wow" before he sat back. She wanted to echo the sentiment. One gentle kiss and she'd fallen off the edge of a precipice. She took a deep breath, trying to slow her heartbeat.

Nicole realized she was falling for Damien Reed, something that should not be happening. It would complicate her life to no end.

"You know," he said. "We can't really date."

She knew it. It wasn't what she'd figured would be the first words out of his mouth after kissing her. Disappointed, she tried to hide it, tried to put on her poker face. There was only one problem. She'd been told again and again that she didn't have a poker face.

"But," Damien continued. "I'm not always going to be your boss."

A flicker of hope brought a slow smile to her face.

He reached again for her hand. Several long moments passed as he moved his fingers across hers. Nicole enjoyed the sensation and waited.

When he spoke, it once again was not what she'd expected to hear.

"Come spend Christmas with me," Damien said.

"Christmas?" She couldn't switch gears that fast.

"Yes. At my home, well, my parent's home. Come spend it with us."

"With you...*and* your folks?"

His lips moved upwards in a lopsided grin. "Yes. I'm asking you to spend Christmas with my parents, my sister and brother-in-law, and myself."

"I-I'm not sure I can get it off. I volunteered to work when I found out I wasn't going home."

He shook his head. "I think your boss can figure out a way."

"Oh! We can't...I mean...you *are* my boss. We're not supposed to..."

He placed a finger on her lips to silence her. "There's nothing in the rules that says I can't invite a co-worker home for a holiday meal. You did mention that Christmas is a special time of year for you, right?"

Nicole remembered their conversation in the cafeteria. That's what he was doing. Taking pity on her. "I don't need you to make my Christmas happy. I'm a big girl and I can take care of myself."

He pulled her hand up to his lips and kissed her palm and she suppressed the shiver of desire that raised the hair on the back of her neck.

"Trust me. I am fully aware of how grown up you are, Nicole Milbourne. I do, however, have no doubt that you will work the entire holiday and try very hard to forget that it's Christmas. Come home with me. I know it won't be the same as with your folks, and I don't know what memories you hold from holidays with your mother, but I bet you'll enjoy my family."

She wavered. She really didn't want to spend Christmas with strangers. Damien did so much out of the goodness of his heart and her mind said that was his reason for inviting her. Her heart prayed there were other, more personal reasons.

"Come because your mother would want you to," he said.

His eyes held hers and she found herself unable to look away. Nicole fought the rush of emotion his gaze brought on. Damien Reed knew too much about her. He knew what buttons to push. What he didn't know was that she hesitated not because of the idea of spending Christmas with strangers. She didn't want to spend Christmas with a man she was falling for with and couldn't have.

He squeezed her hand. "Please?"

"All right," she said. "Thank you for inviting me."

"Good." With that matter settled, Damien attacked his breakfast with relish and the conversation returned to work and superficial topics.

After they finished breakfast and the dishes, Damien waited for her to change and walked her back to the hospital in time for her shift.

"We shouldn't be seen together."

"Why? We're co-workers."

"No. We're not. You're my boss and people will talk."

"Let them. We've done nothing against the rules." They'd reached the emergency room doors and stopped. She wanted to reach out and touch him. To feel his warmth one more time before they returned fully back to their peer relationship. His hand came up as if he wanted to do the same thing, but he tucked both hands into his jeans instead.

"Thanks for the breakfast, Dr. Milbourne. It was," his voice deepened, "exceptional."

Nicole couldn't tear her eyes away from his lips. She followed his lead and stuck her hands deep into her coat pockets before she gave into the urge to grab the lapels of his jacket and pull him to her.

She saw one of the nurses watching from inside. "I'd better go."

Damien nodded. "I'll work out the schedules and let you know."

She thought about protesting the invitation one last time, but clamped her mouth shut, knowing he expected her to argue. "All right," she said.

As she walked away, she knew she'd capitulated not because he'd won, or because she had no other alternative.

She'd given in because, in her heart, she very much wanted to go.

8

A solid week went by with little or no conversation between Damien and herself, other than patient care. Nicole's last nerve was just about gone. Had he decided inviting her home was a mistake? She yanked her lab coat on and headed for Amanda Grant's room.

"Hi, Amanda," Nicole said, working hard to bury her worry and focus on her friend. Since Amanda had been diagnosed with ovarian cancer, the two of them had re-forged a friendship Nicole treasured. The rules stated Nicole couldn't be Amanda's physician, but that didn't stop her from making sure everything looked all right.

She grabbed the chart and dropped into a chair next to the bed. "How are you feeling?"

"Oh, you know," her friend answered. "I've been better." Amanda kept steady eyes on Nicole. Gentle eyes that seemed larger with the absence of most of her hair.

Nicole silently agreed. Her friend looked like she'd spent a year in hell. She'd lost weight. There were deep circles under her eyes. And her skin had turned almost translucent.

She should have rebounded from her last chemotherapy session by now. Nicole opened the chart. Her lab work cleared her for this next chemo session. Just barely. Her numbers were down, but not alarmingly low.

She flipped through the chart. "You should be feeling better than this. I don't understand why you haven't recovered more."

A hand touched Nicole's arm and she glanced up, seeing a quiet resolve in Amanda's eyes that was unsettling. She swallowed. Her friend looked like a woman on a mission. A very sick woman on a mission. Nicole rubbed her arms. Had it gotten chilly in here?

"We need to talk," Amanda said.

An instinct for preservation kicked into high gear and whispered "run" to Nicole. She glanced at her watch. "I'm due on shift in a few minutes. I can come by during lunch." Nicole stood. "I really should get moving. I did want to wish you good luck with today's chemotherapy."

Nicole made it to the end of the bed before the bomb fell in the form of Amanda Grant's soft voice. "I'm not going to have chemotherapy."

Nicole flipped open the chart to the med list. There they were. All the cancer-killing meds were ordered, as well as the palliative medications to help her through the next several days. She looked up. "What do you mean--?"

"I've decided to stop chemotherapy."

"You mean delay it until you feel better."

"No. I mean stop it."

"But that's a...a..."

"Death sentence. I know."

Nicole felt the walls start to close in. She stepped closer. "You can't do this. You're tired. Give it some time. You can't just give up."

"For what? For a few more weeks? Or months? I have stage four cancer. You, above all people, know how bad that is."

Tears pooled in Nicole's eyes and she blinked to clear her vision. "I also know you can't give up hope. They could come up with a breakthrough any day. Even any moment. You haven't given chemotherapy a chance. A couple rounds isn't enough to slow things down."

"No, it's not. But it is enough for me to recognize what my quality of life will be."

While Nicole grew more upset, she saw Amanda's resolve remain constant and that panicked her more than anything. She grasped her friend's hand. "Amanda, I haven't known you long, but I know you're a strong woman. An amazing woman. You're too young to make this kind of decision. You have a lot still to do. Remember all the places you said you wanted to visit? Please. You can't quit."

Amanda pulled her hand out and placed it on top of Nicole's. "I've been through this before, remember? I watched my mother go through all these treatments." She paused before continuing, gripping Nicole's hand tighter. "I know you had a rough time with your mother, Nicole."

"That's got nothing to do with this."

"I think it does. It colors decisions you make when you're close to a situation, like now." She took a deep breath. "You know what I wish. I wish you could be at peace with your mother's death. I want that more than anything for you, my friend. I've seen how good you are at what you do. I've seen you learn what you can give to the world. Now you need to learn how to receive. How to let others into your heart like you've let me in."

Nicole bit her lip to keep from crying. "It hurts too much to let people in."

Amanda nodded. "Sometimes it does hurt. But there's a flip side. A wonderful one that more than compensates for any pain."

Nicole knew there was some truth in what Amanda said, but her heart couldn't handle it. "I—I can't let you do this, Amanda."

"It's not your decision to make. I'm going home, Nicole."

"Today?" She stared at her, confused. "You're being discharged?"

"I'll be in here a couple days for more tests. After that I'm going back to California. I grew up there. I've spoken to my brother and his wife. They want me to come and live with them."

"But that means—"

"We may not see each other again." Amanda's eyes filled with tears. "I hate that part of this decision. You are what I will miss the most. I'm sorry. I don't want to spend what time I have left looking at snow. I want warmth and sunshine."

Tears streamed freely down Nicole's face now. She was being deserted all over again. And there wasn't a thing she could do about it.

Nicole stood and, with supreme effort, found her emotional equilibrium. "I guess, if that's the way you feel about it, there's nothing I can do to change your mind."

"Nicole, I don't want us to part this way. It's not good for either of us, but most especially you. Don't retreat into your shell. You've got a whole new life opening up in front of you. Embrace it."

Nicole swiped at the tears on her face. "Don't worry about me. I'll be just fine. I wish you—" She couldn't say the word peace. It stuck in her throat like salt on a wound. With a gasp, she whirled and fled the room.

And ran smack into Dr. Damien Reed.

He gripped her by the shoulders and steered her into an empty waiting room.

"I'm so sorry, Nicole," he said, pulling her against his chest.

She didn't want his sympathy. She didn't want him to feel bad for her. Or for Amanda. She wanted him to fight. She wanted to fight for Amanda's life.

She pulled back and thumped his chest. "How can she make this choice? She doesn't know what she's doing."

She kept pounding. After several long moments, she collapsed against him. "Why? Why is she doing this?"

"Can you understand that she wants to enjoy what time she has left?"

"But she could double, even triple her time with chemotherapy. Maybe even go into remission."

"The chances of that happening are pretty slim with her diagnosis." He pulled her chin up. "You know that."

She sniffed. "Stranger things have happened. She can't just give up."

"She's not giving up. She's making a choice, empowering herself and taking control of the time she has left."

Nicole heard him. She understood what he was saying, but she couldn't grasp the idea with her heart. "You are better at separating your feelings from things like patient choices. You sound like you've been through this with patients before."

"Once or twice."

The feeling that she was missing something kept nagging at her. She pulled back and looked at him. And saw the truth. "You counseled Amanda, didn't you?"

He hesitated, and then gave a quick nod of his head.

"You convinced her to give up."

"You know me better than that. I only answered her questions as best I could. She made the decision on her own."

"But you *agree* with her choice."

"I *respect* her choice. There's a difference."

Nicole shook her head. "No. There's not. At least, not for me. I would never agree to someone giving up. My mother never gave up. She fought to the end."

"Are you sure about that? Is it possible a ten year-old, well-loved daughter might have been shielded from some of the worst of her mother's disease? From some of the choices she made?"

"My. Mother. Never. Gave. Up. And I can not—*will* not condone anyone's choice to stop fighting." Nicole swiped at lingering tears on her cheek, stood tall and straightened her lab coat. "If you'll excuse me, Dr. Reed, I'm due on shift."

"Don't do this, Nicole," he said, placing a hand on her arm. "Don't shut yourself off again."

She shrugged him off. "It's the only way I know how to survive, Doctor." She walked out of the room wondering if her legs would carry her. Ducking into the nearest restroom, she slammed the stall door shut and crumpled onto the floor.

Damn it all to hell. It was happening all over again. Someone she cared about was dying and there wasn't a thing she could do about it. Nicole leaned back against the stall door and hugged herself, closing her eyes tight against the tears.

Why had she become a doctor if she couldn't save the people who were important to her? Why? Everything felt muddled together. Amanda's choice, Damien's acceptance, visions of her mother in those last few months.

The bathroom felt hot, stifling, confining. Nicole needed out. Out of this hospital. Away from this way of life where she'd believed she could actually help people.

She ran into the hallway. Damien leaned against the wall, waiting for her. She shook her head. "I can't talk to you now."

"Don't shut me out. Let me help."

Nicole signaled with her hand for him to stop. "I don't want to talk to any doctors right now. Least of all, you."

Nicole ran toward the E.R. and out through the doors.

She trudged through the snow in work shoes and lab coat, having left her winter coat back in her locker. It only took a couple of blocks for the sub-freezing temperature to take hold and chill her through.

Nicole dug in her pockets and realized she didn't even have her apartment key. She glanced back toward the hospital and knew she wasn't ready to return there.

A few doors down, she came to the local public library. Hurrying inside, she kept going until she was between bookshelves as far back as she could go. Nicole squatted against the wall, hugging herself like her arms were the only thing keeping her body from exploding, and waited for the shivers to die down.

It took several minutes before her teeth stopped chattering and she could stand without spasms of phantom cold coursing through her body. Even more time passed before she truly felt warm again.

No matter how hard she tried, or how numb she wanted to be, she couldn't run from it any longer.

Is it possible your mother shielded you from the worst of it?

No. She would not have done that. Would she?

I respect Amanda's decision.

But it's not the right one. Is it?

Don't do this, Nicole. Don't shut me out.

I have to. You're helping my friend die. Or...are you?

Nicole winced. Her mind knew she was being unfair. The problem was how to get that through to her heart.

Did my mother shield me? She grabbed a book, any book, and sat down in an overstuffed chair in the corner.

She opened the book on her lap, but the words blurred as she thought about her mother's death. She'd been ten at the time. She remembered hearing her mother at night, trying to hide how sick she was. She remembered creeping into the bathroom, getting a washcloth for her mother, rubbing her back, anything to make the hurt go away.

Then she remembered all the extra times she'd gone to her father's to stay. And the sleepovers with friends.

Maybe her mother had tried to keep the worst of her disease from Nicole. But she'd done session after session of chemotherapy. She'd fought to the end.

Nicole had seen death a time or two since starting her residency. She'd seen the look on patients' faces when the time came. The look of despair on their faces changed to acceptance and, finally, a sort of peace.

She could no longer deny that her mother must have gone through those same emotions. Maybe there had been a point when she'd said enough. When she'd decided it was okay to leave.

Except she left me. Just like Amanda was doing now.

Nicole shook her head. This wasn't about her. She wasn't the one dying. Amanda had the right to make her own decisions.

She hung her head. *Just like my mother did*.

And I didn't make it any easier. That, however, was a wrong Nicole could make right. She closed the book and, for the first time, read the title and chuckled.

The Healing Season: a Christmas to Remember.

Glancing skyward, she wondered how any force could be working so hard to heal her wounds. Wounds she'd never tried to heal by herself until now. She placed the book back on the shelf, saw the time on her watch, and the bottom dropped back out of her world. She'd been gone for hours...while she was supposed to be on duty.

That was a violation of the worst kind. An offense that could mean instant dismissal from the program. Her heart raced faster than her feet as she rushed through the library. She needed to be back at the hospital now.

"Excuse me, miss?"

The voice stopped her. She turned to see a man behind the checkout desk holding out a coat?

"A man dropped this off a while ago. Pointed you out and said to leave you alone, but you'd need this eventually.

Damien! Her hands flew to her face. She'd said some horrible things to him. He'd never forgive her. She threw her arms into the coat, paused to take a long, fortifying whiff of his scent and, with a thank you tossed over her shoulder, rushed out the door.

By the time she arrived at the hospital, her shoes were once again soaked. There was no time to change now. She tossed Damien's coat behind the triage counter and went in search of him.

Before she found him, Dr, Jones found her. "Where have you been, Dr. Milbourne?"

Oh, crap. This was the nail that would seal her fate. Nicole couldn't come up with a single reason to explain her absence. The only thing to do was to come clean and pray the man had some shred of decency in him.

"I—"

"Dr. Milbourne has been out of the facility on a

research project I asked her to follow up on."

Nicole whirled around to see Damien, certain her eyes were about to bug out of her head.

"Are you certain that's the story you want to go with, Dr. Reed? I have witnesses who saw her run out of the hospital in an agitated state. If you are lying, you could lose your accreditation and, with that, everything you've worked for the last few years."

No. Nicole couldn't, and wouldn't, let Damien put his own career on the line for her. She turned back to the attending physician. "I was out of the hospital, Dr. Jones. This is not Dr. Reed's fault."

"There is no fault here," Damien said. "Dr. Milbourne took time I granted to come to terms with a difficult diagnosis."

"No. I left on personal business," she said, turning to glare at him.

"No. You didn't. It was sanctioned time away," he said, locking eyes with her.

"Enough!" They both turned to Dr. Jones. He stood there with lips compressed for several endless seconds. Nicole stuck her hands deep in her hospital coat pockets, crossing fingers on both and praying for leniency.

"I'm not sure what's gone on here today." He shook his head. "And since you two are more interested in saving the other than telling me, I'm going to have to make a decision based on what I know."

Here it comes. All the hard work, the studying, making the dean's list...it was all about to go down the tube. She felt Damien take a step closer, but he didn't touch her. He must know if he did, she'd explode, as keyed up as she was.

"What I know is that each of you has shown abilities beyond your studies."

The ringing in Nicole's ear wouldn't stop and she was having trouble understanding Dr. Jones as he continued.

"I know that you have also both shown exemplary concern for your patients."

That got through. The man was paying both of them a compliment?

"I believe—" He got a pained look on his face. "—that you will both turn out to be excellent physicians in your respective fields. And, since patient care was not at risk, I think we'll consider this matter settled."

He turned to leave and Nicole's shoulders edged down toward normal. Before Dr. Jones got too far away to be heard, he turned back. "Don't let this happen again."

"No, sir." Nicole and Damien answered at the same time.

Nicole watched him until he was out of sight, then turned to Damien. She could see wariness in his eyes and in his straight stance.

"Thank you," she said.

"No problem."

"Um, we need to talk."

He nodded his head.

"But there's someone else I need to talk to first."

His voice softened. "Yes. Go. You and I—" he pointed a finger at each of them, "—have lots of time."

Nicole stopped outside Amanda's room to brace

herself. This would, most likely, be the hardest thing she would ever do. She was going to say goodbye.

Right after she apologized profusely for her horrible behavior. She straightened her shoulders and pushed the door open.

Amanda Grant wasn't alone. A man close to her in age, and with the same auburn color to his hair, stood near the window.

"Oh, I'm sorry. You've got company," Nicole said. "I'll come back later."

"No," Amanda answered right away. "Stay. I'd like you to meet my brother, James."

As they shook hands, Amanda told James that Nicole had kept her sane through these past few weeks. Nicole shook her head, trying to deny it.

"You have been my ally and friend," Amanda told her. She turned to James. "Could you give us a few minutes?"

"Sure. I could use a cup of good coffee, anyhow. The stuff out of the machines isn't much more than badly flavored water."

"Don't I know it," Nicole said.

After he left, Nicole wasted no time. "I'm so sorry."

"No need to apologize. I kind of blindsided you."

"No. You have every right to make the choice that is best for you."

"Yes. But maybe I could have told you in a gentler way."

"And maybe I could have listened to what you were really saying," Nicole said. "I'm a doctor. And part of my training has been to learn how important listening is." A vision of Damien's approving face brought the edge of a smile to Nicole's.

She sat on Amanda's bed and reached for her hand. "I don't know what I'll do without you around to be my sounding board. Who will right my world when Dr. Jones tosses me to the wolves?"

"You'll do just fine. You already have. And don't think my moving to California lets you off the hook. I expect regular updates on how things are going with Dr. Tall, Dark, and Handsome."

"Dr...what?"

"You heard me."

"He's my boss," Nicole said.

Amanda chortled. "He's way more than your boss. I see it in both your eyes. You're in love with the man. And if you don't act on it and snap him up before someone else does, I may just come back and haunt you."

This was the one topic Nicole had kept close to her heart. How could Amanda possibly know? And if she knew, did anyone else?

"The whole hospital is buzzing about you two."

"Oh, no!" A crimson blush heated Nicole's cheeks. "It can't be so," she said.

Amanda laughed. "Oh, yes, sister. A lot of hearts are breaking in this place. They've all come to the easy-to-reach conclusion that Dr. Damien Reed is off the market."

"How will I ever face any of them?"

"With your head held high, that's how."

"He's, um, invited me to spend Christmas with his family."

"You are going, right? You *have* to go, Nicole." Amanda grabbed her arms. "You and I both know from personal experience how fleeting life is. You need to grab happiness while you can. Your mother would want you to."

Nicole felt the bittersweet in her smile. "Yes, she would."

"Then say you'll go. Please."

Nicole nodded. "I'll go."

Amanda settled back into her pillow and nodded. "Good. I think this is going to become another one of your favorite holiday memories."

Nicole had a strong feeling her friend was right.

9

"I can't believe I never asked how far it was."

Now that they were on their way, a serious case of doubt tied Nicole's stomach up in acid-dipped knots. She wrapped her purse strap around her finger, unwound it, and then wound it again.

"Why didn't you mention it was a two-day drive?"

He flashed the lopsided smile that generally got him what he wanted. "Because I knew you wouldn't come with me if I told you. Besides, it's only a day's drive when there's no snow on the ground."

She glanced outside at the white landscape. "So you wait until we are well on our way to tell me this?"

He shrugged, exhibiting not one ounce of remorse. "I waited until turning back would be difficult."

"I have only five days off at the hospital, you know."

"I know. I booked you out. And it wasn't easy, since you'd cancelled your days off. Still, I could have worked it out for seven, or even six days instead of just the five. It would have made it easier."

The memory of yesterday's goodbye with Amanda added to the sour taste in her mouth. She'd looked so at peace, but Nicole knew how bleak Amanda's future was. How could she take this time away when cancer had such a hold on so many people?

"I didn't go to medical school to make life easier for myself, Damien. I went to learn...to stop the disease that claimed my mother's life and now threatens Amanda. I'm here so the Amandas of the world don't have to get what amounts to a death sentence anymore."

Nicole wrung her purse strap even tighter. What was she doing here? She should be back at the hospital, finishing her residency.

Damien glanced at her sideways, sighed, and pulled over to the shoulder. Turning toward her, he stretched an arm across the back of her seat and, with the other one, gently disentangled her hand from her purse.

"I know you want to cure the world. And I applaud your determination to make that happen. But you can't live your life for research, Nicole. There has to be more."

He paused. "Are you really that upset this has become a two-day trip? Because we can turn around and go back."

He sat so still Nicole couldn't even see his chest moving. Was he holding his breath?

Did she want to go back? She should. There was so much to do. Yet the idea of this time away with Damien had worked it's way into her heart. It felt equally as important. Nicole glanced back at the road that stretched out behind them. Yes, she should go back to the hospital. But that wasn't what Damien had asked her. And he had earned her honesty.

"No," she answered. "I don't want to go back."

Damien closed his eyes for a brief moment, then the lines around them crinkled up in that way she'd come to love. He touched her cheek. "I'm glad."

His touch drained any last vestige of guilt she felt at taking this time for herself. She didn't know where this thing between them was going, but she knew she wanted to follow its path, almost more than anything. Not that it didn't scare her. Nothing had ever derailed her goals before Damien Reed came along. Now here she was, heading to Vermont to spend Christmas with his family.

Damien pulled back on the road, got up to speed, and set the cruise control. Then he reached for her hand, pulling it over to his leg and holding it there.

Nicole could imagine no other place she wanted to be at that moment. Tomorrow was Christmas Eve and spending it with Damien felt like a dream come true.

They stopped to eat in a roadside café. When they got back on the road, snow had started to fall again and the wind had a definite howl to it.

"I'm not sure how much further we'll get the way this is blowing," Damien said. White knuckles on the steering wheel belied his casual tone.

Nicole chewed her lower lip. Snow in Seattle was mostly non-existent unless you drove to the mountains.

She'd never traveled any distance in it and she didn't know how he could even see out the window.

"Is this a blizzard?"

Damien chuckled. "Hardly. But it is getting treacherous." He glanced at the highway sign. "I had hoped to get further today but it would be wise for us to stop."

Nicole gulped. "Whatever you think."

"I know a nice little inn a short way from the highway off this next exit. How about we stop there for the night?"

"Sounds good."

It took another half-hour of nail-biting, slow driving for them to navigate their way to the inn. Once inside, it was Nicole's turn to hold her breath. Would he request one room or two?

When he dangled two keys in front of her, she felt palpable relief, along with another, more elusive emotion. Did she want to share a room with him? She shook her head at the new feeling. She'd never...well, there had just never been much time for relationships.

"What?"

"Hmmm?"

"What did you shake your head for?"

She blushed red and mumbled something she hoped sounded like "nothing" as she turned away. He showed her to her room on the second floor and opened the door.

Nicole stared in amazement. The place was larger than her apartment. And a lot better appointed, although not in a pretentious way. An overstuffed couch sat in front of a gas fireplace. Damien flipped the switch to light it and the room felt instantly warmer. Landscapes reminiscent of the northeastern territory dotted walls accented in different shades of beige.

Nicole turned to Damien. "I can't afford this."

He waved a hand. "It's my treat."

She started to shake her head, but he stopped her with a hand on her shoulder. "Please. Let me give you this. Consider it an early Christmas present."

She stared at green eyes that fascinated her, with their myriad of colors. She could get lost in those eyes. She *was* lost in them. And wanted to be for the rest of her life.

The thought brought her up short. This was not good. They'd only just begun to know each other. No way could she afford to start thinking about lifetimes.

"All right. Thank you," she finally said.

She was rewarded with a smile.

"Good. Now, is there anything you need?"

She waved a hand around the room. "What else could I possibly need?"

Damien leaned down to whisper in her ear. "Me?" He'd said it so quietly she wondered if she had heard right.

As he backed away, he asked if she was hungry, which she wasn't.

"Then why don't we take some time to relax and meet up for drinks in—" Damien glanced at his watch. "About two hours?"

Nicole nodded, her mouth too dry to formulate words. When he leaned down and kissed her lightly on the lips, her legs stopped responding to her orders and shook like she'd just finished a marathon.

She closed the door and leaned against it, her hand

covering her stomach to silence the nerves doing flip flops there. She was acting like a virgin, for crying out loud.

She pushed off the door. Hell, she didn't even know if he had any intention, or any interest, in making love with her. Nicole wandered into the bathroom, delighted with the large jetted tub, separate shower and sheer tiled expanse of the room. This bathroom was bigger than her kitchen. She started the tub filling, added some hotel bath salts, and soon settled into the sudsy water.

With closed eyes, she tried to shut out the world. Instead, Damien's kiss took front and center stage. His lips, both gentle and strong, had felt tentative against hers. Searching. As if he didn't know how she would respond.

She felt her response even now deep inside. What would this night hold? And did she want to take this step? She sat up as she remembered. He was the lead resident and it was against the rules to fraternize.

She could be tossed out of the program. Everything she'd been working so hard for would be lost. She had come close to being dismissed once already. She splashed her hands in the water.

She couldn't do it. Even if he wanted to, she couldn't take the chance.

Nicole decided the only thing to do was call him and cancel their meeting for drinks. After hurriedly drying off, she wrapped the towel around her and picked up the phone by her bed.

Except she didn't know his room number. Holding the phone against her chest, she wondered if the front desk could put her through. He wouldn't be happy when she cancelled. After all, she would be spending the next couple days with his family. It would be very rude of her to simply call and cancel.

No, she decided. She'd meet him. And explain in clear terms that she could not jeopardize her career over some dalliance, some minor attraction that would more than likely disappear with the melting snow.

Nicole nodded her head and put the phone back in its cradle. Yes, that was the right thing to do.

She took special pains with make-up she rarely wore.

She sprayed perfume, a gift from her parents, in the air and let it settle over her. Mmmmm. It smelled like a light spring bouquet.

She dug through her small suitcase, tossing clothes on the bed. Nothing felt right for letting a man down easy. Especially a man who fit into his clothes like they were a comfortable second skin.

Finally she settled on the quintessential little black dress. It was demure, with a higher, slightly draping neckline. That it had a bit of sass in a backside that dipped to show no bra was incidental.

That it hugged her hips was lost on her as she enjoyed the swirl of a skirt that fell to mid-calf. Yes, this would work. She looked good in it, but not sexy. Different from work, but not saying come hither.

As she brushed her teeth, she didn't worry about the fact that she took an extra minute or two to make sure they sparkled. She applied a newly purchased lipstick and pursed her lips, well satisfied with both the color and the outline. She had nice lips.

Kissable lips.

Lips that wanted to be kissed.

Nicole sighed, knowing she had to shut that door hard. She glanced at her watch and realized she still had twenty minutes before they were to meet in the hotel bar.

She flipped through a magazine left on the desk, but found nothing of interest. She re-packed her clothes. After all, they would be leaving early in the morning.

Still fifteen minutes to go.

She straightened the bathroom.

Twelve minutes.

Deciding it was crazy to just stand here and wait, she clutched her purse and went on down to the bar.

A tree twinkled with white lights in the corner. Nicole smiled. Tomorrow would be Christmas Eve. Her second favorite day of the year. She sat in a booth where she could gaze at the tree, not minding that it felt secluded and dark.

When the waiter asked her what she wanted to drink, she opted to wait for Damien to order. She set her purse on the table, but soon moved it to her lap.

Taking a deep breath, she tried to formulate how she would tell Damien that they could only be friends. The lights on the tree twinkled away and a wave of nostalgia hit her. Her mother had loved this holiday. Kate and her Dad had, too. She missed them.

This would be such a different Christmas. She was falling in love with a man she couldn't love. Her parents were in the Caribbean. Nicole felt more alone than she had since they'd dropped her off at the airport in Seattle to head out for this residency. She wiped an errant tear from her face just as a hand settled on her shoulder. She didn't jump. She knew it was Damien.

He sat down beside her. Maybe a little too close for friends, but it felt nice so Nicole let it slide for the moment.

"Thinking about your mother?" The question, in his deep, mellow voice, didn't cause the usual rush of emotions she worked so hard to stifle.

"Is it silly to still miss her so much after all these years?"

He settled an arm around her shoulders and Nicole allowed it. After all, he was simply trying to make her feel better. That it felt so good was secondary.

"Doesn't seem that way to me," he answered. "I can't imagine what it would be like to lose a parent so young." He pulled her in tighter for a moment. "I don't want to imagine it at any age."

"I understand that better than I want to."

"It had to be hard. You were ten, right?"

"Yes. I still remember it like it was yesterday."

"Were you there?"

"No." Nicole gave a quick shake of her head. "And I held that against my dad and my grandmother for a long time afterwards."

The waiter set their drinks on the table, red wine for her and some sort of mixed drink for him. She looked at him.

"You were focused on your own memories when I got here. That was pretty obvious." He shrugged. "I took a chance you were a red wine kind of woman and ordered a cabernet I like."

He'd guessed right. She nodded and took a sip. "It's good."

He smiled, and any lingering sadness left Nicole. "Thank you," she said, looking up at him.

"You're welcome."

The strains of holiday music started up and Nicole realized there was a trio in a shadowed corner of the lounge playing music. A couple moved onto the dance floor, close together, and swayed to the slow tune.

Damien nodded toward the floor. "Let's dance."

Nicole shook her head. "I'd rather not."

"Why not?"

"I can't dance."

"Everyone says that. Come on. I promise I won't laugh...or even groan if you step on my foot."

Nicole chuckled. "All right. But don't say I didn't tell you so."

Damien stood and held out his hand. When she took it, they both paused for a moment to stare at their intertwined fingers. Nicole wondered if he felt the same heat flowing through his body as she did.

"Nice dress," he said, his eyes shining with approval.

When Nicole reached the dance floor, she turned to find Damien several steps away. He looked like he had stopped in his tracks. His mouth wasn't outright hanging open, but it was certainly slack. What had caused this reaction?

He regrouped and joined her, cocooning her hand in his as she placed her free hand on his shoulder. When his other hand settled low on her back, she felt invisible fingers of desire wrap around her and settle between her legs. She looked up at him.

Damien's eyes were dark and filled with a smoky desire. "That's—" He cleared his throat and started over. "That's a very nice dress you're wearing."

"Thank you," Nicole said.

"I've never seen you wear anything like this before."

"It's not exactly hospital wear," she said with a laugh.

"No," Damien answered. "It's much...sexier."

Sexier? This wasn't sexier. She hadn't meant to make that impression. Disconcerted, she hid her face in his chest and let him carry them around the floor in a slow cadence with the song being played. She'd never been able to dance well before. With him, it felt effortless.

That was the moment she stepped on his toe. She backed up and apologized.

Damien wasted no time pulling her back into his embrace. "See. No injuries. I think we can survive the two left feet you say you have."

"All right. But don't say I didn't warn you."

Nicole settled her cheek on his chest and gave herself up to the music...and the feel of being in Damien Reed's arms. She felt protected. And, if she was honest with herself, she liked it.

His hand crept up until it rested on the bare skin of her back and all thought fled. He moved his fingers in small motions that were anything but soothing. A warmth spread through her, becoming a heat she was having trouble ignoring.

Was he as affected as she was by this closeness?

As if reading her mind, he pulled her even tighter in to his body and she could feel his hard need. She looked up at him, her eyes wide open with a desire she could no longer hide.

At that moment the music stopped. The problem was, she hadn't stopped. Her body raged with desire for Damien. This would not do. She gave herself a mental shake and pulled away.

"We need to talk."

"I think we may be beyond talking." He reached for her as the strains of yet another mellow song wafted from the stage.

Nicole put both hands on his chest, trying hard to ignore the taut muscles she felt underneath the crisp white shirt and tie. The man looked great in jeans. In slacks and tie, he looked devastating.

Back at their table, he moved next to her, but she put some distance between them, steeling herself against the confusion in his face. She took a sip of her wine and dove in. "We can't be," she waved between them, "like this."

"Like what?"

Was the man toying with her?

"Like this," she said again. "Linked. Romantically."

His brows knit together. "Why not?"

She sighed and took another sip. "You have to understand. All I've ever wanted to do is go into medicine. I want to find cures for the cancers that steal people's lives. I have to."

"Because of your mom," he said.

"Yes. And Amanda, too. And every other woman who

hears the harsh reality of the words 'ovarian cancer'. It's a vocation for me. I can't let go of that."

"There's nothing stopping you from continuing."

Oh, yes, there is. She stared into her glass, wondering how to get him to understand. "You and I dating...it can't happen. I'm so very grateful to you for everything. For your tutelage, for your patience, for inviting me to your family Christmas. But you know the rules about fraternization as well as I do."

The grin was back. "Yes," he said. "I do."

So this—" She motioned again back and forth between them. "—can't happen."

Damien nodded. "Is our working relationship the only reason?"

"Isn't it a good enough one?"

He scooted a little closer to her. "Do you mean you have no other objection to...fraternizing with me, except for work rules."

Nicole grew wary. "That's a pretty significant reason."

He moved closer still. "It would be except for one small flaw in your logic, Dr. Milbourne."

Nicole gulped. "What's that?" She whispered the words as his lips hovered mere inches from hers.

"I'm no longer in the program," he said, his eyes focused on her lips.

"What—what do you mean?"

"I mean, Doctor, that I graduated as of two days ago."

"You...graduated?" She couldn't stop staring.

His grin widened for a moment. "I knew I'd met the program requirements. Did that a couple months ago. I've stayed on...to help out."

"You have? You did?" She frowned, trying to focus on what he was saying.

"Two days ago, I met with Dr. Jones and asked to be formally graduated from the program. He accepted my resignation. So you see, work is no longer an issue between us."

"It isn't?"

She licked her lips and Damien reached up to run a finger across them. "So soft, so kissable. May I kiss you, Dr. Milbourne? May I kiss you the way I've wanted to since I first set eyes on you, fresh and green into the program."

That was when it all sunk into Nicole's conscious mind. He was free of the program. And they were free to explore each other, to see where this thing between them would go.

Could he kiss her? A slow smile spread across her face. "Oh, yes. I'd like that very much, Dr. Reed."

"Please," he said as he touched her lips. "Call me Damien."

10

One tentative touch. That's all it took for them to realize the crowded bar was no longer where either of them wanted to be. That first taste became an instant aphrodisiac and Nicole wanted more.

Much more.

Yet when she would have rushed to their room, Damien strolled. She had to admit that her arm linked in his while they waited for the elevator felt nice. It felt comfortable, like she belonged there.

Once in the elevator, he covered her hand with his. "Are you certain you want to do this?"

"Oh, yes," she said, reaching with tiptoes to pull him down for a long, lingering kiss. "More than anything."

Damien wove his free arm into her hair, pulling her closer.

"Ahem."

They broke apart, seeing the doors open and an elderly gentleman standing there waiting.

Both Nicole and Damien mumbled apologies as they traded places with the man.

"No apologies needed. Have fun," he said with a twinkle in his eyes.

The doors closed and they both burst into laughter.

Damien recovered first. "I haven't been caught making out in, well, a long, long time."

"That's a new one for me, too," Nicole said, wiping her eyes.

Damien ran a finger along her face. "You've smeared your makeup."

Oh no. Nicole's hand flew to her face. "I must look crazy."

Damien lifted her chin. "You look beautiful."

Nicole shook her head, unable to speak.

When Damien spoke again, there was a sense of awe in his voice. "You really don't know how beautiful you are, do you?"

She felt the blush and knew it was visible when he smiled.

"Come on. Let's get that stuff off your face."

Once inside her hotel room, Damien lifted her up to sit on the bathroom counter. Then, using a warm washcloth, he gently wiped the cosmetics off her face.

"Absolutely beautiful," he murmured, as if talking to himself. Then, he combed his fingers through her long hair. "You don't know how many times I wanted to pull the pins out of that bun you always wear. To see this gorgeous hair fall around your shoulders and to run my fingers through it."

Nicole sighed as he massaged her head. This felt better than, well, just about anything. He leaned in and kissed her forehead, then moved to her temple. With his hands still tangled in her hair, his lips wandered down her face. By the time he reached the corner of her lips, Nicole couldn't stand it anymore and turned to meet him.

A touch of whiskey enhanced the spicy flavor of Damien Reed. She opened her lips to taste more of him, letting her tongue reach for more.

Wrapping her arms and legs around him, she pulled him in tighter, moving her arms up and down his back, enjoying the muscles that moved as he tilted her head back to reach her neck. It took very little to un-tuck his shirt and feather touches along the beltline of his slacks had him groaning.

He straightened, Nicole coming with him as he renewed their kiss. She wrapped her arms tightly around him as he moved and she soon felt the bed underneath her.

Damien leaned over her, an arm on either side, and kissed her again. Then he moved to lie beside her. She reached for him, but he stopped her. Instead of kissing her lips, he pulled the draped material away from her shoulder and began to pepper kisses along her collarbone.

Nicole felt the brand of each kiss and welcomed it.

When he drew her dress down further and Nicole knew no bra stood in their way, she began to chew her lip. She'd never been, um, amply endowed. Would she be enough?

He glanced up and smiled. "You are everything I

dreamed you would be."

Nicole gulped, and then returned his smile with one of her own. He kissed her then, and she melted against him. When he moved to the still-clothed dip between her breasts, she shivered in anticipation.

His hand, resting lightly against the underside of her breast, began to move. Up, over, around, she arched with an ache she'd never known before. When he grazed her tight nipples with his thumb, she almost screamed.

"I'm never going to make it if we keep going like this," Nicole said, surprised at the huskiness in her voice.

Damien chuckled. "I want to enjoy this." He kissed the swell of her breast. "Every last minute of it."

He lowered her dress to bare a breast and took a nipple in his mouth. Nicole reached to pull him in tighter, begging him to take more of her. She tried to unbutton his shirt, but they were too close. She didn't want him to stop, but wanted to reciprocate.

He must have sensed her frustration, because he pulled back and edged off the bed. She took the hand he held out and stood. He turned her around and moved her hair over one shoulder. As he kissed her shoulder, she felt a tingle settle low in her back. When he moved to her neck and she felt the dress's zipper slide open from waist to buttocks, the shiver moved around to her belly to settle low.

The dress slid to the floor. Now she stood in nothing but a tiny pair of black underpants. A case of nerves set in again. This was the moment of truth. This is where she'd turn around and see. Either he liked her body or she'd catch that fleeting look of disappointment before he covered it up.

She turned slowly, taking a step back to put some space between them, staying focused on his eyes.

Eyes that held her gaze without wavering before drifting lower. And lower still until they reached her toes, then started a slow meandering rise back to her face. She watched him grin. Not like a man trying to seduce her, but like a boy in a candy store.

Nicole relaxed. He wanted her. She knew that now without a shadow of a doubt. When he reached for her, she stepped closer and nudged his arms to his sides.

One button at a time, she opened his shirt and then peeled it back. It joined her dress on the floor. Damien reached for her and she held him off. "You said you wanted to take it slow, right?"

He groaned. "Leisurely is one thing. You're going to kill me."

She ran both hands across his chest. She liked the smattering of dark chest hair. Not too much, just the perfect amount. Moving down his arms, he made it until she reached his hands and he grabbed for her.

"Uh uh. Not yet," she said laughing. She unbuckled his belt and tugged on it until it was free, tossing it over her back. The zipper of his slacks came next. When she started to slide them down, he grabbed her hands.

Lifting her, he settled her back in the middle of the bed, shrugged out of his slacks and joined her.

He then spent the next several minutes getting to

know her body better, kiss by molten kiss. Always near, but never touching where she needed him to. When he finally dipped his hand beneath the lace, her body met him halfway and she begged for release.

"Not yet," he said, pulling back. "I want us to crash over the top together this first time.

"Then you'd better catch up."

He patted the lace, a finger slipping deep into the vee and it was Nicole's turn to gasp.

"I can't take much more." She kissed him and began her own exploration. She ran her fingers through the curls on his chest, well satisfied with the shudder that coursed through him. When she trailed her fingers down the line of hair on his abdomen, he held his breath.

"Breathe," she said with a wink. "You're going to need the oxygen."

He jerked as she feathered her fingers along his shaft. She watched, out of the corner of her eye, and a part of her wondered...he was so...

"We'll fit just fine," Damien whispered in her ear.

More than ready to find out, she grabbed him and he gasped. "I think," she said, "it's past time to test that theory."

"You are so right." He grabbed the ready condom and sheathed himself, raised over her, and paused with a look that said more than words to her. It seemed almost like...could he be looking at her with love in his eyes? Nicole shook her head.

"No?"

She smiled. "Not no. Yes. Yes, yes, yes."

He held her gaze as he entered her, taking his time, and she gasped as he filled her.

"Okay?"

"Very okay," she answered, then wrapped her legs around him as they moved in harmonized rhythm.

About the time she couldn't take it anymore, he groaned and moved faster. And faster. She matched his pace. And his desire.

In only moments, she felt the explosion of her climax as he let loose with his own. Even then, he didn't stop, keeping up slow, measured movements. She was surprised when the passion rose again, crashing into another crescendo of mind-numbing sensation.

He leaned on his elbows as they both gasped their way back to normal. When he rolled back to her side, Nicole approved wholeheartedly as he pulled her into his arms. She played with the hair on his chest as it rose and fell, his lungs still searching for a normal rhythm. Her own breathing struggled along with his.

Minute after minute, their bodies came down from the high of making love and drowsiness replaced wonder in Nicole's brain.

"That was amazing, Doctor," Damien said.

"Please," she said as her hand slowed its motion on his chest. "Call me Nicole."

His chuckle was the last thing she remembered as she drifted off to sleep.

"Nicole?"

"Mmmmmm." The voice filtered in, but didn't make

sense. She'd been having the loveliest dream and longed to return to it. She'd been wrapped in Damien Reed's arms as they made slow, languorous love. Even in her sleep she knew turned on when she felt it.

"Come on, sleepyhead," the voice said again. "Time to wake up."

Funny. It sounded like Damien, but it couldn't be. He was still in her dream. Then fingers caressed her cheek and she remembered—everything. As a lazy smile spread across her face, she opened her eyes to the grinning face of her lover. And the man she would now, and for always, be over-the-top in love with.

"Welcome back to the land of the living," he said. "You don't wake up easily, do you?"

"Only when I'm having a dream I don't want to let go of."

He raised his eyebrows. "So, you were dreaming about me, were you?"

"Maybe. Maybe not."

"I think you were."

"Well, a woman's got to have some secrets." She stretched muscles still trying to wake up, raising her arms overhead to get maximum effect.

In doing so, the sheet that draped her slipped and Damien took advantage of the opportunity, kissing first one breast and then the other. "You have the most kissable breasts," he said.

Trying to think straight as need coursed through her, she shook her head. "They're too small."

"I disagree. From my vantage point, they are perfect."

He cupped one in his hand and nuzzled it. "Absolutely perfect."

When he pulled a nipple into his mouth, Nicole decided to stop arguing with him. Except that moments later, he leaned away from her. She reached for him, but he shook his head. "I wish we had time. But we've slept longer than we should have already. We've got just enough time to shower and grab a bite to eat, after which we need to get on the road. It's Christmas Eve."

Her eyes widened. It *was* Christmas Eve. She hadn't even realized it. They needed to get on the road to his parents' house. She ran a hand lightly down his arm, wondering if maybe they should just stay here for Christmas. After all, he'd look pretty good in a big red bow—and nothing else.

"Don't even think about it," he said with a laugh.

"What?" She tried for a look of innocence.

"As much as I would love to spend Christmas in bed with you, my mother would kill us. Now go...you can have the shower first."

As she tumbled out of bed naked and headed for the bathroom, she glanced back, satisfied that he at least appeared regretful.

Moments later, steamy water calming her body, she was still having trouble putting their night's lovemaking into perspective.

She would meet his parents in just a few hours, and if she couldn't squelch the idea of dragging Damien back to bed, she'd ruin what was beginning to feel like a very

108

important first meeting.

The shower curtain shifted and a naked Damien Reed stepped in. Nicole shrieked as he reached for her. "What are you doing? You said we didn't have time."

He shrugged. "I figure if we shower together, we're saving time, right?"

She cocked an eyebrow and felt passionate warmth fill her anew as he reached for the soap.

After a hurried breakfast and a call to his parents, Nicole and Damien got back on the road. The countryside sparkled with white, but at least it had stopped snowing. The plows had also been through, so with the road in better shape, they made good time.

As they turned down the drive to the home Damien had been raised in, Nicole gulped. The driveway was lined with snow-laden trees and seemed to go on for miles, like something out of the movies. Her nervousness increased with each tree they passed. Damien hadn't told her much about his home, or about his family. If the driveway was any indication, they lived in a mansion and he was filthy rich.

She gulped again. She'd never been around people who had a lot of money. She had no idea how to act.

Finally, they rounded one last corner and pulled up in front of a modest home. It was larger than anything she was used to, but surprisingly unassuming. A combination of brick and natural cedar shake siding, it looked built to meld with its surroundings instead of stand out. Along each window, a draping evergreen garland with small, white twinkling lights enhanced the effect of a warm, country home and Nicole sighed with happiness.

Damien opened her door and held his hand out. She took it and stepped out, glancing again at the house.

"Don't worry. My folks won't bite."

She smiled. "It's funny. A few minutes ago, I needed that reassurance. But this house...I don't know, it just feels...likes it's welcoming me."

He nodded with a smile of satisfaction. "I feel that way every time I come home."

Then the front door opened and a man and woman came out to greet them.

Nicole could not stop herself from staring at Damien's mother. Even with the gray starting to pepper in and the shorter style, the color was reminiscent of her own mother's hair. Plus she had a smile that felt as welcoming as her outspread arms. Damien Reed's mother wrapped those arms around Nicole and, for a moment, she was transported back in time. She was ten years old again and on the receiving end of her mother's hug.

Nicole returned the hug with a sense of happiness she hadn't felt for a long, long time. When she pulled away, she knew there were tears in her eyes and she didn't care.

It was hard to explain, but somehow, Nicole felt as if she'd just come home.

11

Once inside, Damien helped Nicole off with her coat. As he hung it up, she took a moment to glance around. Christmas was everywhere. Every wall, table, doorway was decorated, yet it didn't overwhelm. It wasn't all lights and shiny objects. It was more wreaths and evergreen, muted ribbons, and other country décor.

The ambiance had a welcoming feel to it and Nicole embraced it. She wandered around the large living room and ran her hands along the garland adorning the fireplace. Damien's mother even had stockings hung. Seven of them. They had that amazing hand-quilted look to them. She smiled at the one with "baby to be" safety pinned to it. She fingered the one with Damien's name on it. It looked old, like it had maybe been his from childhood.

Next to it, a much newer one hung with the name Nicole stitched on it. She ran her hands along it as Damien wrapped his arms around her.

"Mom insisted. She called me to make sure she had the spelling of your name right and sewed it just this week."

Nicole tried very hard to keep the wobble out of her voice, but didn't quite succeed. "It was very sweet of her." Turning into his arms, she buried her face in his chest to hide the sheen of tears.

"Ahem."

Nicole jumped at the voice and tried to pull away. Damien only laughed and held on tighter.

"I'm not interrupting anything, am I?" The twinkle in his father's eyes set Nicole's mind to rest. Separating herself, she looked at Damien. "I need to thank your mother."

He nodded his approval as his father responded. "She's most likely in her favorite room in the house—the kitchen." He crooked a finger to show her the direction, but she didn't need it. She could follow the wonderful smells.

"Mrs. Reed?"

"In here," she called.

Nicole rounded the corner and stopped in her tracks. Where every other room was low key, comfortable, and country, the kitchen was huge and modern. Stainless steel appliances and granite counters gave way to the only country accent in the room—hickory cabinets.

"Wow," she said.

Grace Reed laughed. "You like it?"

"It's beautiful."

"And very functional. This was the one room I didn't care if it conformed to the rest of the house. My husband would like me to hire some help, but I love to cook," she said as she waved a hand around. "And this is my therapy room."

Nicole's eyes shone. "My grandmother would have loved this. She was always baking."

Grace patted one of the stools that bordered the central island in the kitchen. Nicole sat down as Grace ladled a cup of steaming liquid from a pot on the stove.

"Spiced cider. My own recipe," she said.

"Mmmm," Nicole said as she cradled the cup to warm her hands and sniffed. "It smells wonderful. Thank you."

As Damien's mother went back to kneading what looked like bread dough, Nicole asked if she could help.

"Maybe later, dear. Right now, all I have left is to get this bread rising."

After some companionable silence, Damien's mother spoke up. "I understand your mother passed away when you were young?"

The question caught Nicole off guard and she felt her body clench in a knee-jerk reaction.

"I'm sorry. I shouldn't have asked," Grace Reed said.

"No. It's fine. I just...I don't know why I still react this way. It's been eighteen years since—" She gulped. "Since Mom passed away. I should be over it by now." She set the shaking cup of cider down before it spilled. Grace wiped her hands on a nearby towel and reached to cover Nicole's.

"You never get over it. And you shouldn't. You loved your mother and missing her is part of that, even after all these years."

"You—" Nicole cleared her throat and tried again. "You

sound like you know."

"I do," Grace said. "I was a little older than you. My mother passed away when I was fifteen. I have learned to live with it. That doesn't mean I don't miss her to this day."

Nicole gripped Grace's hands and they stayed there for several long moments sharing private memories. When Grace pulled away to go back to her bread, she patted Nicole's hands.

Nicole spoke first. "I think she's the reason I love Christmas. It was her favorite holiday. She went overboard every year, to the point of bordering on corny." The memory cloaked her in warmth. "I always loved it."

"The good memories are the ones we treasure forever."

"Thank you," Nicole said. "I wish I had the words to explain how much I appreciate the stocking you made for me."

"You're welcome, dear. I want you to feel at home here."

"I do already."

"Good. Damien says you want to go into research?"

"Yes. Cancer research."

"Is that because of your mom?"

"Yes. She died from ovarian cancer."

"That's a nasty one. I had a good friend pass away a couple years ago from the same thing," Grace said.

Nicole took a sip of cider. "It is. And only nineteen percent are caught at stage one, where it's treatable. I'd like to increase those odds and find an early warning system."

"We certainly need it," Grace said, then paused. "I've

only just met you, so feel free to tell me to go jump in the lake. But I need to ask. Won't you miss patient care?"

"No, I don't think so." Memories of those early weeks and how tough interaction with patients had been for her morphed into more comfortable moments. She'd never expected to like that end of things. It wouldn't sway her choice to go into research. But maybe she would miss it, just a bit.

"Damien says you have a knack for solving riddles."

Nicole smiled, pleased at the compliment.

"He also said you were very good with the patients."

Nicole chuckled. "He's stretching the truth with that one," she said.

"Stretching what truth?" Damien asked the question as he entered the kitchen. He sniffed the cider, reached for a cup and poured himself a ladleful, settling next to Nicole at the counter. Their knees touched and Nicole could feel the heat pass between them.

"You told your mother I was good with patients?"

"You are," he said without pause.

She looked at him, incredulous. "You've got to be kidding me. I'm a wreck with patients."

"You were at the beginning, but you got past it. You're great with them. Really." His brows knit together. "Don't you know that?"

She thought about it. It had gotten easier. In some cases, she'd found it quite easy to discuss symptoms and treatment with patients.

"Maybe," she said. "But I don't have your ability. You walk in a room and the patient feels better. You know patients and nurses alike call you Dr. Charisma behind your back, don't you?

"No!" He laughed. "And I believed I had my nose to the gossip scent. How did I miss that?"

Nicole laughed. "No one ever called you that outright? I'm amazed."

"Not even once," he said.

Nicole laughed when Damien shook his head, once again taken with the fact that the man did not fathom just how good-looking he was.

"It also," she continued, "helped you with the patients. That smile of yours disarms them when you enter the room."

Grace laughed. "We've always considered our son handsome, but it's nice to hear that from someone else."

Nicole glanced at Damien, and then turned for a second look. Did she really see a tinge of red creeping up his neck? Was the man actually embarrassed? That was a first, and she had to admit she liked it.

Damien cleared his throat. "Maybe this would be a good time to show you to your room," he said getting up.

His mother laughed. "Dinner will be in an hour, so don't be gone too long."

When she winked at Damien, Nicole felt the deep flush hit her cheeks. Could his parents know they'd spent the night together last night?

As she followed Damien upstairs, she wondered about the arrangements for their stay here. He wouldn't try to put them in the same room...in his parents' home. Would he?

He opened one of the doors off the hallway and she

entered a room that was decidedly feminine. A white four-poster bed with eyelet lace was accented with blue and rose pillows. Posters of nineties rock stars adorned the walls and a corkboard over the chest of drawers was pegged with photos and award certificates.

Nicole looked closer. High school sports. Sarah Reed seemed to excel in distance track events and in long jump.

She turned to Damien. "Sarah?"

"My baby sister," he said.

He'd mentioned a sister and brother-in-law. And the extra stocking in the living room meant she was pregnant.

"Sarah got married last year and they live about two miles away, so her room is pretty much the spare bedroom these days."

Nicole nodded. She cocked her head as she looked at Damien. "Any other family I should know about?"

He laughed. "No other siblings. A couple of aunts and uncles, none of which will be here for the holiday. Oh, but Sarah's pregnancy? She's very pregnant, as a matter of fact. I believe she's due in late January."

"With the first grandchild, I presume? Your mother must be thrilled."

"She is. And I'm indebted to my baby sister for taking the heat off me."

"To give your folks grandchildren?"

"Yes. I'd rather do it on my own timeline instead of to satisfy my mother's raging grandmother genes."

"She knows how gorgeous your children will be," Nicole said and then realized what she'd said. "I—I mean, when you have kids...I'm sure they'll be cute...sweet...you know, whenever you get married and have kids, that is."

Lame cover-up, Nicole. Really lame.

Damien reached for her but held her at arms length. "Hmmm," he said, giving her a critical once over. "Seems to me we'd make some pretty good-looking kids together."

Nicole felt the world slow its rotation. She could see the eyelet canopy swaying with air from the heat vent, but it moved in slow motion.

Damien kissed her. Not with the passion of last night, but with a sweeter, more endearing feeling. His lips moved over hers as if he cherished every touch. Already certain she loved Damien Reed, she knew now she would never love anyone else with the depth of emotion she felt for him.

Her arms traced the muscles of his back, reveling in the fact that, for however long this would last, she could touch him like this.

Reality returned in the form of a door crashing open downstairs and a very feminine "hello-o-o-o" reverberated throughout the house.

Damien let go of Nicole and she stood waiting for a wave of dizziness to abate. He turned to the window and muttered something about timing.

Nicole joined him and he put an arm around her shoulders as they watched Sarah and her husband unloading food dishes and gifts from the car.

"I need some distance from you or I'll never be able to go downstairs."

"What do you—oh!" The implications of what he said hit Nicole. "Ummm, all right. I could unpack?"

He nodded. "That would be good. I'll...unpack, too.

Give me a few minutes and we'll go downstairs together."

Nicole smiled. "I'd like that."

He kissed her forehead and was out the door in a flash.

12

Nicole unpacked and wandered around the room, taking time to learn a little bit more about Sarah. She had to be close to Nicole's age, but what an overachiever. The diploma for her master's degree in education was framed on one wall and two class pictures filled with kindergarten children graced the wall beside it.

It was obvious Sara would make a great mother. Damien would be a good parent, too. This family seemed to foster that. Nicole wondered if she had the patience to raise children. She stood in front of the full-length mirror and swayed her back to round her stomach. She'd be a cute pregnant person. But could she raise a child? That took a lot of work.

And a lot of time. She frowned and straightened. She'd never imagined having kids. Her career had always been her goal and having children would change that. She touched one of the class pictures.

"I can't give up," she whispered. "I need to make a difference. I need to find a cure."

Laughter floated up from below just as she heard a knock on her door. "Ready?" Damien said.

"Uh, sure." she answered. She couldn't quite shake the feeling that she stood on the edge of some precipice. She tried. She shoved thoughts about babies to the back of her mind and planted a smile on her face as she turned.

"You okay?" Damien asked.

With a quick nod, she answered. "I'm fine." She widened her smile. "The real question is, are you?"

He took her hand. "As long as I don't get too close to you, I will be."

His comment wrapped her with a warm spirit that seemed completely in line with how this house, and this family, made her feel. It also did wonders to dispel the melancholy that had begun to settle on her shoulders.

They barely got through the kitchen door before a whirlwind threw herself at Damien. Sarah Reed-Campbell was a petite woman, dark-haired like her brother, but that was where the similarities ended. Where he was quiet and composed, she demanded attention just by entering a room.

"Damien!" she squealed as she continued to hug him. "I've missed you *so* much." She backed up and tapped his chest. "You need to come home more often, big brother."

No one escaped Sarah's attention, as she next wrapped her arms around Nicole. "It's so good to meet you. You're as gorgeous as my brother said. And I'm so glad you got him to come home for Christmas. He probably wouldn't have come if not for you. He's so wrapped up in his patients that he rarely leaves that hospital." Sarah nodded. "You, it seems, are a good influence on him."

Nicole barely kept up with Damien's fast-talking sister. Still, she learned some important tidbits of information from Sarah's one-way conversation, one of which was that Damien had told his sister she was beautiful. An unwarranted blush filled her cheeks at the second-hand compliment.

She also now knew he didn't come home often. She glanced at Damien and was surprised to see him squirming a bit under his sister's barrage. So the man had dodged a holiday or two because of work. His devotion to medicine rivaled her own single-mindedness. Nicole wondered how their respective careers would allow for raising a family. Maybe he didn't want children.

He placed a hand on his sister's bulging stomach. The animation on his face quickly put to rest the idea that he would not want kids.

Sarah still had not stopped talking.

"Sis, put a cork in it," Damien said. "Take a breath and give someone else a chance to talk."

Sarah stopped, but didn't look a bit sheepish.

Damien introduced Nicole to Sarah's husband, Mark, and the family went into dinner preparation mode, with Sarah giving orders and everyone following them.

"It's easier to just let her have her way," Damien whispered to Nicole.

"She's a powerhouse, isn't she?"

"She is that," he said, watching her hand the platter of prime rib to Mark.

"I like her. She's fresh and natural and she makes folks smile."

"Definitely," he said. "Just don't tell her I said that."

"Said what?" Sarah came around the corner.

"That you're a brat," Damien countered.

"Of course I'm a brat. That's what little sisters are supposed to be, aren't they?"

Between Grace's talent in the kitchen and Sarah's organizational skills, they were soon seated at the dinner table with their plates laden with food. Conversation flew as they dished up. It felt like meals back home. Having grown up with a houseful of foster kids, noisy mealtimes were the norm for her. Nicole hadn't realized how much she'd missed it until now.

Was this what she wanted? A house full of family? Is this what Damien would want? She glanced at him as he bantered with his sister. Would he be willing to be with someone who wanted to wait to have children until she'd accomplished her career goals?

"Earth to Nicole," Damien whispered.

"Sorry," she said. "Day-dreaming, I guess."

He frowned. "You sure you're all right?"

No. I'm not. She and Damien had just started dating. It was too soon for her to be thinking about all this. She needed to let it go.

"Really. I'm fine," she said.

He gazed at her for another long moment before she saw his nod of acceptance.

Damien's father tapped his glass and stood as everyone quieted. "Christmas is a time of celebration on many different levels. Tomorrow, we celebrate Christ's birth. Tonight, we celebrate family. It's good to have all of you here. Our children—" He tipped his glass in turn to Damien and Sarah, then to Mark. "Our soon to be born granddaughter, and now Nicole, whom I feel certain we will see more of. Welcome to our family. Merry Christmas, everyone."

They all sipped their drink of choice. Nicole used the moment to try to get her emotions under control. She felt so welcomed by this family it was almost overwhelming.

Damien patted her knee under the table and she looked up at him and smiled as everything else faded away.

Later, they all dressed and went to midnight services, something Nicole had never done before. Her father and mother had always opted to go Christmas morning and then rush home for a big breakfast. It felt different, but not foreign. The church was decorated in trees and light. Sitting here felt calming and right. Having Damien's arm along the back of the pew offset that calmness and Nicole worked hard to concentrate on the services.

Afterwards, Sarah and Mark headed out with the promise that they'd be over in time for breakfast and gifts in the morning. Damien drove Nicole and his folks back to the house, where his parents retired almost immediately.

Damien poured a glass of wine for each of them and they settled on the couch to stare at the lights of the Christmas tree.

"How are you enjoying this Christmas?"

"Oh, Damien. I'm loving it." She turned to him. "You know my holiday looked rather bleak. You saw that and made it so much better than I could ever have imagined. Thank you for that."

"Then you're happy here?"

I'm at home here. "Yes. Your family has been great." She stared at the tree. She felt so welcomed, in fact, they had her re-thinking goals she'd held close to her heart since childhood.

Damien twirled a strand of her hair between his fingers. "I'm glad. I wanted you to like it here."

I like it so much, it's scary. "I do." She turned to him. "Something your sister said makes me think you don't come home every Christmas."

"I do come home for Christmas. They'd like me to come home more often."

"But your career is important to you."

He agreed. "There are always patients to treat. You know more than anyone how hard it can be to get away."

Damien didn't catch the hushed strain in her voice as he remained focused on her hair. "You probably don't want children when you marry, then. So you can focus on your patients."

"Not necessarily," he said, pulling a strand of hair to his nose and inhaling. "I think it's possible to have both."

"I don't see how," she mumbled, feeling the chasm widen between them.

He leaned in to nuzzle her neck. "I love how the pulse in your neck starts to race when I kiss you here. And here. And here."

Her body said enjoy, but her mind was racing and wouldn't stop. She pulled back. "You know how much going into cancer research means to me."

"Uh uh," he agreed, pulling her sweater back to gain access to her collarbone.

"I don't think I could have kids. At least not for quite a while. I'd need to reach my research goals, first."

She felt him pull back as it finally registered that this was something important to her. "You mean you want to find a cure for cancer before you can think of having children?"

"It's been my focus for years."

"Why can't you do both?" he asked. "I could have a medical practice and still raise a family. Why not you?"

"Because research means long hours."

"So we switch off duties between the long hours and the family stuff. Except at first, of course. I can't carry the baby, give birth, or recover for you."

"Exactly." She winced at the raised tone of her voice. "We can't even consider it until I'm further along in my work."

"That a bit ridiculous, don't you think?" He ran his hands through his hair. "Why are we even having this conversation, anyhow?"

"Because I see how good you are with kids. How much you enjoy even your sister's pregnancy. I don't know if I could give you that...give any man that."

"Why not?" His voice powered up to her level and Nicole stiffened.

"Nicole, is this really something we have to sort out

now? This holiday is important. Why can't we simply enjoy it? We're friends, right?"

Her mouth went dry, all thoughts of procreation gone in an instant. After what they'd shared, he considered them only friends? "Friends?" She croaked the word out, afraid to try to say more.

"You know what I mean," he said.

She pushed him back and stood, waiting for the pain running through her heart like an electrical current to ebb. It didn't. "You see us as friends with benefits?"

"No. I think we're much more than that."

"So did I," she said.

"What's the matter?"

"Just so you know, Damien. I don't sleep around."

He shook his head and his eyes registered surprise. "I didn't think you did."

"Sleeping with you was more than just a 'friends with benefits' thing for me."

"It was for me, too."

"Well, that doesn't seem to be the case based on what's coming out of your mouth."

Now he looked really confused, but she didn't care. "I'm going to bed," she said and fled up the stairs.

In her bedroom, she collapsed onto the bed. What had she been thinking? That the man might actually love her?

She began to throw her clothes in her bag and then realized there were no taxis out here in the country. Pulling back the window shade, she saw it had started to snow again. How was she going to leave?

She slumped onto the bed and crumpled into the fetal

position. Damien didn't love her. She should be happy about that. It ended her quandary. She could go on with her research goals and not worry about relationships and families and...and children.

She clutched her stomach. So why was she so miserable? Unable to find a way past a despair that made her heart hurt. And how would she endure spending Christmas Day with a man who did not return her love.

Changing into a nightgown her parents had sent her in an early Christmas package, she walked over and stared out at the snowy landscape. Had it only been a few hours ago it had seemed so cheerful and homey?

When she heard a soft tap at her door, she padded over and opened it. Damien stood there, still fully clothed. And looking decidedly haggard.

"Can I come in?"

"Why?"

"Please? I need to talk to you. And I can't do it out here."

"Why not?"

"Because my parents are sleeping across the hall, for one thing."

She didn't want to let him in, didn't want to have the conversation they needed to have. Yet some perverse side of her opened the door wider. She left him to close it and walked back over to the window. She turned, ready to beat him to the punch, but stopped short.

Damien had not moved from the closed door. He stood there with wide eyes and his mouth hanging open. That's when Nicole glanced down and saw how diaphanous her nightgown was, especially with snow-light streaming in through the window.

Let him look. Let him see what he'll be missing. She had the satisfaction of seeing his Adam's apple bob up and down. Damien reached for a throw blanket and held it out to her.

"I think you'd better put this on so I can have a clear head. Apparently, being aroused by your nearness muddles mine and I say the wrong thing."

She wrapped the blanket around her and went to sit in the window seat. When Damien settled across from her, she tucked her feet up under her. Touching him would be too much to bear.

"I said the wrong thing earlier."

Nicole started at him.

"You know, downstairs? By the tree?"

"Yes. I know."

He laid a hand on her knee, but she stiffened so he pulled it back. "I'm sorry."

Nicole shook her head and sighed. In her heart, she knew he was sorry he couldn't return her love. And she didn't have the heart to make him suffer because of it. "I know you are."

His smile was tentative. "Good. I don't want us to fight. I want this Christmas to be special."

This Christmas would definitely stand out as the most memorable one she'd ever had. Nicole wished the deep ache in her chest would go away. It was too hard to be close to him and not be with him.

Then he smiled and her heart broke in two. "It's only a

few short hours until morning and we both need some sleep." He stood and kissed the top of her head. "Thanks, honey. I don't want you upset, and I'd like us both to enjoy tomorrow."

After he closed the door behind him, Nicole laid her head in her arms and let the tears flow. Tomorrow would be the hardest day of her life.

13

A few sleepless hours later, Nicole heard motion in the hall as someone made their way downstairs. She got up and stared into the mirror at bleary, tear-streaked eyes, wondering how she'd ever make herself presentable.

After a long shower, she dressed in her favorite holiday skirt and sweater, applied some makeup, and prayed it would hide her all but sleepless night. Pleased with how well her efforts worked, she squared her shoulders and prepared to endure what would probably be the longest Christmas Day of her life.

She took the gifts she'd brought down to place them under the tree. It wasn't much. Seattle coffee for the Reeds and a little something for Damien. Following the smell of brewed coffee to the kitchen, Nicole found Damien's mother dressed and quietly preparing breakfast.

"Merry Christmas," Grace said, stopping long enough to hug Nicole.

Tears stung her eyes, but she willed them away and hugged the woman back. When they separated, Grace gave Nicole a long look. "Did you sleep well?"

Nicole shrugged. "Well enough."

"Is everything all right?" Worry was evident in her voice.

Nicole put on what little of a poker face she had and reassured Damien's mother that all was well.

"Good." She patted Nicole's cheek. "There should be no sadness on Christmas."

Nicole nodded, afraid her voice would break if she agreed out loud. "Can I help?" She waved at the counter.

"Definitely," Grace said, handing her an apron. "Why don't you finish up the bacon and sausage? I've already got the ham cooked and potatoes in the oven. I just need to finish the eggs. By then, Sarah and Mark will be here."

They had just about finished preparations when Damien and his father walked in. His dad went straight for the coffee pot, while Damien went first to Nicole and leaned down to kiss her cheek in greeting.

If she stiffened a little, it was just to help remember to keep her distance. When he frowned, she knew he'd felt it. Too bad. He'd have to get used to some boundaries.

Damien poured a cup of coffee and took a slow sip.

They all turned at the sound of the front door. "Merry Christmas," Sarah called, rushing into the kitchen.

"Mark's putting the last of our presents under the tree. I promised I'd bring him coffee." She poured a cup, started to walk out of the kitchen, then turned back to them. "Come on...let's go unwrap gifts!"

Grace laughed. "We should eat breakfast first."

"Aw, come on, Mom. You say that every year."

"And every year you talk me out of it."

"Then it's settled. We open gifts first. Besides," she continued, her hands enfolding her stomach. "You're not going to make your grandchild wait until after breakfast, are you?"

Even Nicole had to laugh at the lopsided logic Sarah used. Still, everyone grabbed their cups and followed her to the living room. Nicole sat in one of the overstuffed chairs, thinking Damien would not be able to sit next to her that way, but he thwarted her plan and perched on the arm of the chair. With his hand resting on the high back of the chair, she couldn't move without touching him in some way or another. And every touch singed her heart even further.

"So, who gets to go first?" Sarah asked, wagging her eyebrows at her brother, who groaned.

"You are horrible at keeping secrets, sister."

"Well, if you'd get on with it, there wouldn't be any more secrets to keep."

With a disgusted sigh, Damien set down his coffee cup and stood up.

"So I get to hand out the first gift?"

He looked at each member of his family and waited as they nodded their heads. Nicole was confused. It was as if they knew something she wasn't privy to.

Damien reached behind the tree and pulled out a small box, holding it behind his back as he turned to Nicole. "I considered doing this in private," he said.

She frowned. Doing *what* in private.

"But family is important to you, right?"

She nodded, glancing at the eager faces of his parents and his sister, still not comprehending what was going on.

"I know that Christmas carries strong memories of your mother," he said.

Nicole jerked her head back around to stare at him. Why was he talking about her mother?

"I hoped this might be a way that her memory could share this moment with us."

When he went down on one knee and held out the jeweler's box, Nicole's heart skipped about three beats before hitting the wall of her chest and breaking through.

"Nicole Milbourne, I've been in love with you since I first walked into that patient's room and you bobbled the swab kit you were holding. Earlier, if I were truthful. At orientation it took everything I had to keep from asking you out right then and there."

She gulped, not able to fully wrap her mind around what he was saying. Hadn't he called them friends with benefits last night? No, that had been her. Had she misinterpreted his words?

"I would have preferred to meet your parents before asking you this," he continued.

Was this really happening?

"But I did speak to your father on the phone before they left on their cruise."

"You spoke to my f-father?" she asked. "When?"

"I called him the day before they left."

"You've—you've been planning this for that long?"

"Longer. And, in case you're interested, your father

gave me his blessing."

He leaned in to whisper in her ear. "Don't worry about the kids thing. We work well together. We'll figure it out."

She could feel tears sting her eyes as her heart thudded inside her chest. When he reached for her hand and placed it against his own chest, she felt his heart racing along with hers.

"I can't imagine a life without you. Will you consent to marry me, Nicole Milbourne? Will you spend the rest of your life with me as I want to spend the rest of mine with you?"

"I-I thought you only wanted to be friends." She still couldn't quite wrap her head around the idea.

He glanced at his parents, then lowered his voice. "I never wanted to be just friends." The gleam in his eyes validated what he said.

Nicole's heart filled with the love she was now free to feel and to show. She could feel his heartbeat beneath her hand. She poured all the love she felt for him into her voice.

"My heart matches yours beat for beat. It always has...and always will. I love you."

"And?"

"Yes," she said. Then again, she whispered. "Definitely yes."

"Halleluiah!" He pulled her up and swung her around in circles. When her feet found ground again, his family surrounded them with hugs and congratulations.

"Well," Sarah said after things settled down. "I doubt anything will outdo that gift, but how about we open the rest of these wonderful boxes."

Nicole settled back into the chair, this time more than happy to have Damien sitting beside her. His arm along the back of the chair now comforted her. His other hand only left hers long enough to open a gift or allow her to open one.

When he handed her another gift, it surprised her.

"A ring at Christmas should stand alone," he said. "That wasn't your gift, it was mine."

She glowed. "It was the only gift I need."

"Go, ahead," he said, pride evident in his voice. "Open it."

She unwrapped a frame. It was a majestic photo of Mt. Rainier. She touched the frame, nostalgia washing over her. This wasn't just any picture of the mountain. The meadow in the forefront was in high spring and alive with the purples and yellows of wildflowers, with the mountain in the background holding on to the white of winter.

It would always remind her of home. She raised eyes filled with love to Damien. "Thank you," she said.

He leaned down for a kiss. "You're welcome. But that's not all. Turn it over.

She did so, and found an envelope on the back. Opening it, she saw a receipt for a significant donation to the American Cancer Society...in memory of Celia Milbourne.

Her mother.

She clutched the paper. "It's too much," she whispered to Damien.

"We all chipped in." Damien waved his arm at his smiling, nodding family.

"I'm...humbled. Thank you so much."

Grace rose and set a hand on Nicole's shoulder. "We know how much your mother meant to you. And that you've had a happy life with your father and step-mother. Now, you have more family. And, hopefully, another mother to love."

Nicole stood and gave Grace a hug that was tight and heartfelt, at a complete loss for words.

After that, the gift opening hit high gear. When Nicole handed a package to Damien. "It's not much." She glanced at the ring adorning the third finger of her left hand. "Certainly nothing as precious as what you've given me."

He opened it and found a photo album, hand-decorated with the words "Dr. Damien's kids". He looked at her and she could tell he didn't get it.

"You still intend to go into general practice, right?"

"Yes. I believe it's where I'll be most useful."

She touched the book. "It's for all the babies you'll help bring into the world."

He spread his hand over the book and smiled. "I like that idea." He looked at Nicole. "I like it a lot, actually."

She blushed as the meaning of his words sank in, then slapped his arm. "First things first. You may be graduated, but I still have a residency program to get through."

"True." Damien covered her hand with his. "You're going to be a great researcher."

"Yes," she nodded. "I am."

"And, when you're ready," he whispered, "we'll talk about kids. Okay?"

Breakfast that morning rivaled any holiday memory

Nicole held in her heart. When Grace and Sarah shooed her away from dish duty, she wandered into the living room and stared at the Christmas tree. She reached out to touch a crystal angel hanging from one of the limbs, feeling more than ever that her mother was here with her today. Here celebrating in the season. Here to witness the birth of a new family.

Damien's arms circle her waist and he pulled her into his chest. "Happy?"

"Oh, yes. More than ever."

"Me, too." They stood there, quietly staring at the tree for some time. "I wish I'd known your mother," Damien said into her ear.

"I wish you had, too." Nicole turned in his embrace. "You kind of do, though. There are a lot of similarities between your mother and mine."

"Then I know I would have loved her."

She twined her arms around his neck. "She'd have loved you, too. You know, I always believed she was what was missing in my life."

"Having a mother?"

"Not necessarily. Kate did a great job of raising me. I know that. But I always had to share that love with all the foster kids she cared for. I thought...I thought that if I could just go back to the small family I started out with. Just me and my mom...that I'd know again the safety and joy of true family."

"And now?"

Nicole smiled up at him. "Now I understand better. It's not the size of the family. It's the love you give to it and that it gives back to you. I had that with Kate and Dad. I was so focused on the memory of my mother, I didn't recognize what I had." She frowned. "I did Kate a disservice. I've never called her 'Mom' and that's exactly what she's been to me all these years. I just refused to accept it."

"When I spoke to your father, she was also on the phone. Her happiness for you, for us, was very apparent. Kate loves you very much."

Nicole snuggled into Damien's embrace, feeling the last pieces of her life puzzle fall into place. "You know, I think we will make beautiful children."

He laughed and squeezed her tight. "When we're both ready, we definitely will."

"I love you so much it scares me," she whispered into his chest.

"I know what you mean," he answered, his breath rustling her hair as he spoke. "I've never felt this way before."

He tipped her head up and lowered his face to hers. "We'll figure our way through it all together."

"I like that idea."

He kissed her then, a kiss filled with gentle promise. Nicole felt forever in his touch and returned it with all her heart and soul.

EPILOGUE

Nicole watched the flurry of activity around her. It seemed silly to make this much fuss, but here they were. Her mother was trying to get Hailey's dress over her head and the three-year old simply would not cooperate.

Shaking her head, Nicole remembered the aftermath of that Christmas three years ago. Her father and stepmother had stopped over on their way home to congratulate her on the engagement...and to officially meet her fiancé. They'd brought their own news. Fate drove them right by an orphanage and, upon visiting, they'd fallen deeply in love with then six-month old, auburn-haired Hailey. Nicole now had a little sister.

Damien's mother was zipping the dress of a very pregnant Sarah, who kept a careful eye on her already dressed three-year old son. Mark, Jr. and Hailey had been inseparable since her family's arrival two days ago. Inseparable...and holy terrors. Nicole sent a prayer to heaven that twins did not run on either side of the family.

Everyone bustled around and she almost laughed at the chaos. All for a single moment in time. It seemed so silly. Today didn't matter. The fact that she and Damien had the rest of their lives together, that was what mattered.

And that attitude had gotten her into trouble more times than she could count over the past several months. With her Mom. With Grace. And with Sarah.

She figured if it was so important to them, let them plan it. But they would have none of it. They'd gotten together behind her back and schemed to involve her, spiriting her away on girls' weekends here and there to shop for dresses, to check out caterers, and to look at cakes. The type of planning that wasn't easy to achieve when they lived on separate coasts.

So here she sat, professional makeup starting to itch on her face. She'd drawn the line at a hairstylist, preferring to leave her hair down in simple curls, just the way Damien liked it. Of course, it would be hidden by the veil they'd talked her into, but at least that was a simple piece that hung from a small banded tiara.

She picked at a piece of fuzz on the white sweats she wore, a gift at the surprise wedding shower they'd thrown her two nights ago. She'd been vehemently opposed to any parties. The women in this family didn't quite seem to understand that she just wanted to be married to Damien.

Very soon now she would get to walk down that aisle with a church full of peoples' eyes centered on her and her alone. She could feel the sweat forming on her skin. Wondering again why they hadn't eloped, she saw her mom shooing everyone out of the room.

"It's time, honey. Let's get you dressed," she said.

Nicole stood, the feeling of being led to the guillotine strong. Did all brides get this nervous about their wedding day? For these same reasons?

She stripped off the sweats praying this day would be speed by. Slipping her arms through the skirt and into the sleeves, the soft whoosh of the satin as it settled over her had a strange calming effect.

She'd chosen an all-satin strapless dress that had a lace overlay with long sleeves. Nicole stood patiently as her mother buttoned up the dress.

When she turned, Kate had tears in her eyes. "You are such a beautiful bride, Nikki."

"Thank you, but you're my mother. You're prejudiced."

Her mom shook her head, turning Nicole toward the mirror. "Look for yourself."

Nicole stared at the image that looked back at her. The white...they'd talked her out of ivory...really did make her skin color glow in contrast. The makeup was artfully deceptive. Her eyes looked larger, her cheeks more prominent, and her lips perfectly shaped. Yet it all looked very natural.

Even the veil framed her auburn hair and made it appear effervescent.

Nicole felt like a princess going to her first ever ball. She turned to see Kate with a wistful smile and tears in her eyes.

"You're mother would have loved to see how beautiful you are right now," Kate said, giving Nicole a careful hug.

It was Nicole's turn to go misty. She set her hand on Kate's arm. "I'm sorry."

"For what?"

"If I ever made you feel you weren't my mother. You were, you know. You taught me what I needed to know to get to this day. You stepped into," Nicole gulped, "some big shoes without complaint. And all I ever did was give you flack for it."

"Is that what you think?"

Nicole nodded.

"Honey, I knew the relationship you had with your mother was a very rare and precious one. I never felt slighted or second best. Our relationship was different, and that's how it should be. I always believed you loved me. And I've always loved you."

"I do love you, Mom." Hugging again, they both dabbed at their makeup and made a pact—no more crying today.

A soft knock on the door heralded company. Her mother went to answer it, then slipped out as Nicole's father stepped inside. And stopped short, his mouth gaping open.

Nicole smiled as she watched him take two big gulps of air. He gulped a third time before he found his voice. "I can't believe this is my little Nikki," he said, his voice breaking.

"I'm the same little girl, Daddy."

"No. I don't think you'll ever be the same again. But that little girl who loves to make everything right, she's inside you." He took both her hands. "I'm more proud of you than I can say, sweetheart." Spreading her arms, he continued. "I can't believe my baby's about to get married."

Nicole nodded through the sheen in her eyes.

"And a fully accredited doctor to boot. Dr. Nicole Milbourne."

She shook her head. "Soon to be Dr. Nicole Milbourne-Reed."

Her father smiled. "I like that you kept your mother's name."

"Me, too. It's kind of like she's here, you know?" Nicole swallowed. "Like she's still a part of my life?"

"She always will be, Babydoll. She always will be."

The strains of music selected as a prelude to her entrance wafted through to them just as the wedding coordinator opened the door. "It's time."

Nicole walked out on her father's arm and watched as the wedding party moved into the church two by two. Finally, it was her turn to move into place. She gazed in awe at the yards of tulle, twinkling lights, and the church filled with people. It looked like a fairytale.

Maybe this formal wedding thing wasn't such a bad thing after all.

And at the front of it all, standing tall and handsome in his black tuxedo, stood the reason for all of it.

Damien Reed. Her love. Her friend. Her life.

Nicole glanced up at the rafters. "See Mom. I'm going to be just fine." A ray of winter sunshine filtered through, as if in happy response.

Then the music changed and Nicole stepped forward into her new life.

THE END

PRICELESS LOVE
by Lavada Dee

1

Taylor pulled into a parking space in the little town of Laurelville. The GPS placed her a mile from her destination. While she could hardly wait to see her friend, she was also reluctant to give up the complete freedom that she'd felt since leaving Seattle this morning. She felt like she had entered a new world, one away from the stress of her life in Manhattan. One she could get used to.

She wasn't tired. There hadn't been any rush so she had taken the time to really enjoy the trip over the Cascade Mountain Range. The red, yellow and orange colors of fall mingled with the evergreens giving the mountains a rich vibrant landscape. The trip through upstate New York and into Maine was famous for its fall color but the Pacific

Northwest rivaled it for beauty.

Taylor glanced at her watch. Caroline wouldn't be home from work yet.That left her time to walk along main street and get a bite to eat in the little café she could see about two blocks away.

Taylor smiled at the scene in front of her. The street could have stepped out of a fifty's movie. Parking ran at a slant and there weren't any meters. When Caroline had written about her hometown, Taylor had formed a mental picture not far off from reality. She strolled past Nash's hardware store, where according to Caroline; you could buy anything from appliances to a hammer and nails. J.C. Penney's took up almost half a block with a Five and Dime store covering the rest.

Everything was perfect, absolutely perfect.

2

Taylor took out the e-reader she carried in her purse. Unlike at home, reading for the pure enjoyment of it seemed natural here. Even eating alone didn't seem so bad with a good story to keep her company. Throwing her usual eating habits aside she ordered a bacon cheeseburger, fries and a cup of coffee. At the first bite, she almost moaned. *I don't know if I'll ever go back to salads for lunch after this.*

As usual she pretty much shut out the world when she was reading a good story, but when she heard one of the men in the booth behind her laugh, it radiated through her. And, now she couldn't shut their low pitched conversation out.

"I'm telling you Pete, I'm not going there. Good grief, it would take less than a day for it to get all over town."

"So what do you care? You said you were looking to get married, get a mother for Mandy, and get a life. I'd think it would be a plus if it were to get around town that you're back on the market."

Taylor heard the man answer. Intrigued, she leaned forward. His voice was a rich deep base; feeling like a voyeur she glanced down at the e-reader, but still his words penetrated her concentration.

"Alright, that does it. I won't discuss this with you anymore. Cripes, you make it sound like I'm a piece of meat."

She could almost see the two men as first one then the other erupted in laughter. A second later the booth shifted as they slid out of their seats. Still laughing, they made their way to the cash register, and she got a good look at them. They were both tall, dressed in jeans and denim jackets, good looking. Caroline was right, this part of the world produced men that, until now, Taylor had only seen adorning ads.

* * * * *

Still chuckling Gabe left the café with Pete. He had an appointment back at the veterinary clinic in an hour. The morning had been spent in farm calls. Whenever possible he arranged his day to include out of clinic time. One of the good things about a rural practice over the city one he'd started in was that a big part of his practice was out in the field.

Pete motioned to his truck. "Got to run, let's do this again. Soon."

Gabe nodded and swung into his own truck. Pete and his wife Georgia, friends since high school, had formed a foursome with Gabe and Bonnie.

Bonnie, he mentally counted off the time since her death. Almost 3 years. It didn't seem that long and yet in ways it seemed like a lifetime. At first he'd been overwhelmed, a three year old daughter, and starting a new business, had all combined to keep him busy.

This impromptu lunch with Pete had him feeling unsettled. But lonesome? Hardly! With six year old Mandy and his family living on the adjoining property how could any man feel lonely? And yet an ache around his heart had him thinking it was time to think about a relationship. He missed being married. He missed sharing the day to day stuff with someone.

He turned the CD player up. Maybe it was Pete's talk of dating, or his friend's happy marriage, or hell, maybe even his sister's upcoming wedding. Whatever, Gabe shook his head. Too bad prospective wives didn't grow on trees. Wanting and finding the right woman were two different things.

Darn, speaking of weddings, he'd better get his rear in gear and cut those autumn branches his sister had asked for. She would want to start decorating the church and if he didn't get cracking he would be in the dog house with the two women he already had in his life.

3

You have arrived at your destination. Taylor let the
tinny voice of her GPS guide her into the entry to Lynch
Ranch. She'd only seen the few pictures Caroline had
emailed her, but the scene felt familiar, almost like she was
coming home. Envy, like a deep hunger shot through her.
She longed for the family and unconditional love Caroline
spoke of. Instead she had a father she couldn't please and a
mother too wrapped up in herself to pay any attention to a
daughter.

Taylor let the car idle so she could get a better look.
The drive was long and paved. She had a vision of Amanda,
Caroline's little niece, learning to ride her bike on this road.
Over the past six years she and Caroline had been emailing
back and forth. It felt like she knew the Lynch family
intimately, as if she'd lived a parallel, albeit long distance,
life with them. She had been there, through Caroline's
emails when Amanda was born. Caroline had shared the

families Christmas's, her first day teaching third grade. The mile stones mounted until they formed a warm safe haven for Taylor. One she held close in her heart.

She put the car in gear and drove up the driveway. Would the reality of being here measure up to what she pictured? Could a family like Caroline described in her emails really exist? Maybe she shouldn't have come; maybe she shouldn't have let Caroline talk her into being in her wedding. Taylor caught her bottom lip in her teeth, a habit that infuriated her father and one she had tried for years to correct.

Then it was too late for second guessing. The car rolled to a stop and Caroline launched herself off the full wide porch. All fears evaporated as the years and distance fell away. They were again like their last time together, two nineteen year old girls on an Alaskan cruise.

Talking a mile a minute, Caroline stopped only long enough to catch a quick breath. Taylor felt the stress in her shoulders relax and a happy chuckle bubbled up inside her. Again, she had the overwhelming feeling she was home and everything was perfect, absolutely perfect.

4

Gabe finished with the last of his four legged patients. Six o'clock, he needed to gather Mandy from the reception area and get home. He sighed, the evening stretched ahead but first dinner and quality time with his daughter. That was the easy part. It was afterward when she went to bed that he dreaded. Maybe Pete was right, maybe he should look into Internet dating. He could specify the location, like thirty miles away. Would that be far enough to avoid his neighbors finding out?

He took off his lab coat and stepped into the front of the clinic. Mandy looked ready to burst through her skin. "What's up, bumpkin? You ready to go and get some dinner going?"

At six, his daughter was still small for her age. At first he had worried that she had inherited her mother's heart issues but tests proved that wasn't the case. His own heart swelled with love.

Mandy ran and gave a leap so he could swing her up. "Daddy, can we go meet the princess?" Her eyes sparkled. "Aunt Caroline said I could, but that I had to ask you first."

"Princess?" Thinking his sister had promised a trip to the movie theater, Gabe was surprised. With her wedding to get ready for, and her friend from the east coast coming, how in the world had Caroline managed to find time for a movie?

Mandy nodded, sending her curls bouncing across her face. He reached over to push the hair from her eyes. "Whoa, what princess?"

"She's there now. I saw her car come in." Her little lip pouted out. "But I couldn't see her. Pleeese Daddy, let's go to Grandma's and meet her."

Gabe waved to Kelly, the receptionist and office manager, and took Mandy's hand. "If Aunt Caroline's friend just got here, they will want to visit. Maybe tomorrow."

"Noooo, Aunt Caroline said I could meet her today." She walked beside him until they got to the front porch where she dug her little heels in.

Gabe looked down at his daughter. Sweet natured, he knew he was blessed with her sunny disposition. This behavior was unusual for her.

"Daddy, Aunt Caroline said . . ."

"And, I said, maybe tomorrow." His voice came out harsher than he intended and Gabe rubbed his hand across his mouth. Squatting down he pulled Mandy into his arms. "Come on honey, Daddy's tired. Let's get dinner started."

A tear rolled down her cheek and Gabe felt his heart turn over. She wasn't demanding, and rarely asked for much. She'd even stopped asking for a kitten. This wasn't right, she deserved better. He was thankful his parents were so close and Caroline had been a god send since Bonnie had passed away. Still, he knew it was time to get his life in shape. It was time that he provided a home and family for his daughter, or baring that, at least a live-in nanny. Things were changing. With his sister marrying and his dad retiring, it was past time for him to provide for his daughter's needs and stop relying so heavily on family.

Mandy still looked like a little thunder cloud when he filled a plate of Mac and Cheese for her. "Come on, it's your favorite."

Mandy wouldn't look at him, but she climbed up on her chair and bowed her head. "Thank you for our food. And, thank you for helping Daddy take care of the puppies and kitties today." She paused and let out a long exaggerated sigh and continued. "And please make Daddy let me go see the princess. Amen."

Gabe bit back a smile and echoed, "Amen." A short rap on the door and his father's voice had him adding, "Thank heavens." Grandpa could always make things right with his little granddaughter. No matter how big or small the problem he always knew what to say.

"I smell dinner in here."

Gabe pushed up from the table but his dad motioned him to stay put.

"Grab yourself a cup of coffee and a plate and join us. There's plenty." His dad shook his head. Well mac and cheese out of the box, no surprise his dad declined.

Everett Lynch pulled up the chair next to Mandy's. "I'll just help you out. It doesn't look like you're doing so good."

"Daddy won't let me go see the princess."

His dad looked over at him and raised his brows. "Princess? You mean Caroline's friend?"

Mandy nodded her head. "She's a princess."

His father covered his mouth, hiding his smile. "Well now, I don't know about being a princess but she's certainly pretty."

"You seen her?" The little girl brightened up like a light bulb.

"Yep and let me tell you, you can't get a word in with Aunt Caroline and her talking a mile a minute."

She turned and gave her grandfather a sad woe is me look. "I want to go meet her."

"I know you do but she's going to be here for a couple of weeks. Let's give Aunt Caroline tonight. I'm thinking of spending the night down here with you and your dad. If you get up early enough we'll walk up in the morning and you can meet her before you and Aunt Caroline leave for school."

When Grandpa talked, Mandy listened and even as bad as Gabe knew she wanted to meet the princess, she nodded in agreement.

"That's my girl. Now eat up that dinner and I'll beat you in a game of Candyland."

* * * * *

Gabe turned down the TV when his dad came downstairs. "Did she go to sleep?"

"Yeah, and can you believe with only one story?"

Gabe liked putting Mandy to bed but he happily shared with his parents. Tonight he'd been more than ready to relinquish bedtime. He rubbed his temple where one hell of a headache pounded.

His dad headed for the kitchen. "Want one of your beers?"

"Yeah, that would be good." He didn't have more than a couple a night. Vets, like human doctors, were on call twenty-four-seven.

His dad gave a grateful sigh and leaned back in the second recliner. The two were silent as they enjoyed the beer. Finally Gabe broke the silence with, "So, she really princess material?"

Gabe's question hung in the air for a few seconds as his dad seemed to ponder an answer. "Welllll, she's something. But a princess, I think not." He again let silence fill the room. "I was serious with Mandy. I'll bunk out in your spare room if it's okay. I'm betting it will be a late night up at my place. In fact it may well be the beginning of wedding chaos, not that we haven't already been in it." He gave an exaggerated sigh. "Just that tonight it seemed to ramp up."

Gabe laughed. "And, you love every bit of it. You love seeing Mom and Caroline so happy." Taking a drink of beer he changed the subject. "Are you ready for retirement? Only a little over a month to go, right?"

"I'm thinking I might be making a mistake taking it in the winter."

"Plan that trip to Arizona. Maybe rent a condo for a couple of months."

"And, what about Mandy. With Caroline newly married you'll be needing your Mom's help a bit more."

Gabe put his beer down on the end table. "You know Dad it's time I stopped relying so heavily on family. You, Mom and Caroline . . . well." How could he find the words, how did you say thank you for all the hours, all the support, all the love?

His dad shook his head. "That's what family is all about, Son. And, we get far more than we give."

"And, it's time I started giving back. You and Mom need to travel, and do the things you've been waiting for retirement to do. I need to build a life for Mandy and me." He laughed and said, "Besides if I don't get to dating, Pete is going to start helping me."

At the thought his dad chuckled. "Horrors, not one like the last woman he brought by."

"You know what he came up with today? He wanted me to join an online dating service. Said it's the modern way to get acquainted . . ."

Still chuckling, his dad said, "And, you said?"

"You don't want to know." He took another drink before saying, "But now I'm having second thoughts. The key word being 'thoughts'."

"Yeah, I hear you. But if you never go out, never accept friend's invitations, never . . ."

"Are you saying I'm a stick in the mud?"

His dad took a long pull from his beer before answering. "I think you need some 'me' time. You work too hard, with the veterinary practice and at being a dad."

Gabe leaned back in his chair. "I am going to do some

changing. First, I'm going to start looking for a nanny/housekeeper. Preferably to live-in which means an older woman, so don't go giving me 'the look'."

His dad laughed. "What look?" With that he handed Gabe the empty and said good night.

Gabe watched as his father disappeared up the stairs. Quiet again descended and with it a feeling that something was missing. Damn, it had to be all this wedding stuff, and couples and . . .

5

Taylor watched the little girl and her grandfather come up the drive. Amanda was talking a mile a minute, while Mr. Lynch indulgently nodded and responded here and there. She was looking forward to meeting her in person.

A smile spread across her face as she watched. Sunshine poured down on the two but Taylor could see the air was crisp by the puffs of smoke from their breaths and Amanda's red cheeks. She turned toward the door as they entered the kitchen. Good thing, because Amanda immediately launched herself at Taylor, giving her a welcome hug. "I wanted to come see you last night but Daddy said I had to give you and Aunt Caroline a chance to talk. Did you get all talked out?"

Taylor laughed and hugged Amanda back. "All talked out . . . noooo, that will take a lifetime." At Amanda's disappointed look she quickly added, "But we got all the really important stuff talked out. Now we'll need you to help us with the rest."

Her words put a smile back on Amanda's face and words bubbled out of her mouth. "I told Daddy you were a princess."

"You did? Did you tell him you were one, too?"

Amanda nodded her head, making her short braids dance. "He says only sometimes, other times I can be a terror."

Again Taylor laughed. It felt so good. Good to be in this home, good to be in this place so unlike where she lived. She bit back the 'poor little rich girl' scenario that leapt into her mind. Some would envy her living in a penthouse, having a live-in cook/housekeeper and a driver. In fact most would want her life. What they didn't realize was that as rich as her life was in material things, it was devoid of warmth and caring.

Mr. Lynch crossed over to the counter and poured himself a cup of coffee. Holding up the pot he motioned to Taylor's empty one. She smiled at him. "Thank you."

Amanda was still chattering away, he shook his head. "Sorry. If it's any consolation her father and I have sore ears from last night and this morning. By the way, what's this thing about being princesses?"

A flush crept over Taylor's face. The princess image was not an adult one she would have chosen for Caroline's father and brother to have. "Oh that. About a year ago Caroline was introducing Amanda to the computer and she found this online educational game. It was set up so I could play it with them from Manhattan."

Mr. Lynch snorted but his smile took any sting out of his words. "Not that kids now days need any introduction."

Taylor nodded. "Probably not, but there can be advantages to computer games. In this game you solved mathematical problems and word meanings to reach levels. The ultimate goal was to get to the highest level and become a princess or a prince."

Amanda giggled into her hand. "I beat Taylor and Aunt Caroline and got to be the first princess."

Warming to the subject, Mr. Lynch said, "When you got your crown or, um, tiara, did you help them?"

Amanda bobbed her head up and down. "Yep, they were right behind me."

Taylor took Amanda's hands in her own to get her attention. "I brought you something."

Amanda's eyes sparkled. "A present?"

"Uh huh, I can give it to you now but you will have to wait until after school to use it. Or we can wait and . . ."

Amanda's eyes widened and she lowered her voice in seriousness. "I'll only take a peek. Then I'll be all ready when schools out."

Taylor laughed, when had she laughed so much? "Okay, it's on my bed in a sack with a pink bow on it." The pink bow had seemed important when she'd bought the harem pajamas in New York. She'd added a princess hat with a veil and a wand from a Disney display at the Seattle airport.

The little girl didn't waste any time and in seconds quiet settled over the kitchen. "You have a wonderful granddaughter Mr. Lynch."

"You're right on that count and its Everett, Mr. Lynch is way too formal.

Taylor heard Amanda and Caroline as they came downstairs with Amanda still talking a mile a minute. A few seconds later a beaming little girl attired in the hat and veil entered the kitchen with the big sack bumping behind her.

Caroline poured herself a cup of coffee and winked at Taylor. "Where's ours? Don't we get princess hats and wands?"

"You can share mine, Aunt Caroline."

Caroline hugged the little girl. "Thank you, and did you remember to thank Taylor?"

Mandy whirled around, and hugged Taylor. "Thank you, I think I will be tired tonight and need to go to bed early. Aunt Caroline said I would need to take a bath before I put on the pretty pajamas."

Talk and laughter flowed around the room for the next few minutes. Caroline brought it to a halt when she glanced at her watch and announce it was time for school.

* * * * *

Gabe let himself into the quiet kitchen. His mother had stopped at the clinic earlier to let him know that she was heading into town to do some errands and she would pick Amanda up from school on her way home. It was three o'clock and thankfully he was done for the day. Tomorrow was Saturday and the clinic was only open until noon. He needed to drive up to the ridge and cut some fall foliage for Caroline's wedding decorations like he'd promised.

He took a deep breath. His mother's kitchen, unlike his own, always smelled of home. Again he vowed to make some changes.

His mother hadn't said anything about Caroline's friend. Maybe she'd gone to school with Caroline and Mandy. Family took priority in Laurelville and school welcomed visitors. In his book, it was another plus for small towns.

He wandered into the living room. With any luck he could catch a short nap in his dad's recliner before everybody came home. He sat down and started to tip the chair back when he caught movement out of the corner of his eye and saw . . . a princess. She looked like she'd stepped out of a dream but he hadn't had time to fall asleep.

She looked as dazed as he felt. Her eyes, held his. Green, they were framed by dark lashes that made them look luminous. Her hair coiled in a severe style and he clenched his hands against the urge to run them through it. What would it look like messed up? She swung her legs off the sofa and sat up. Color flooded her face, making her even more beautiful, if that were possible.

His words were soft, almost a whisper in the quiet room. Even so, they sounded almost like a violation to him. "I'm sorry. I didn't mean to wake you. I didn't realize anyone was home."

She smiled and he drew in a deeper breath. It felt like the first one he'd taken since seeing her. No wonder Mandy was calling her a princess. Jeans looked sexy as hell on her but he'd bet she'd look good in anything. Or . . . nothing. He shook his head, and silently warned himself to get a grip.

Finding his voice he said, "By the way, I'm Gabe.

"Glad to meet you Gabe, Caroline's brother right? I am her friend from the East Coast, Taylor Hamilton."

She pushed herself to her feet, and he registered long legs and all the right curves to go with them. He immediately shot out of the chair to stand up with her. Motioning to the kitchen he said, "Can I get you something to drink. Coffee, iced tea . . ."

Again she smiled. "Thank you. I didn't mean to fall asleep. East Coast time must be messing up my internal clock."

"Jet lag, I've heard it can be lethal."

"Usually it doesn't affect me but then I don't have such relaxing free time to indulge in the luxury either."

They made their way into the kitchen and Gabe put on a pot of coffee. "Do you travel a lot?"

"Not as much as I used to. Work keeps me busy."

Gabe was surprised. If he'd given it any thought he would have guessed that her time was her own. From the designer jeans to the soft sweater and pearls, she looked like money.

So now what to say? He stalled, taking down a couple of mugs. "How do you take your coffee?"

"Black, especially when it's fresh. I have to use cream at the office."

"Office? For some reason I got the impression from Caroline that your office was a prestigious law firm." Why hadn't he paid more attention to his sister when she'd bubbled with news about Taylor?

Taylor chuckled and at the sound he almost dropped the cup he was pouring coffee into. Something about her was playing havoc with his libido. And, he was enjoying it. It had been too long since he'd conversed with a beautiful woman if the tightness in his jeans was any indication.

Her words brought him back to earth and reality. Again he reminded himself to ease off. This wasn't like him and she was Caroline's friend.

Seemingly unaware of his reaction she said, "I do, I mean, I work in my father's law firm. And, I guess it is pretty upscale, but I was referring to my real job." She held up her fingers in quote marks at the word 'real'.

Gabe poured their coffees and sat down at the table with her. "This sounds interesting. And, I take it the coffee is . . . interesting too."

She laughed and almost seemed surprised at it. "I work in a . . . sort of free legal aid office. Kind of like the health clinics that are run with volunteers."

Now this he hadn't seen coming. He was stopped from commenting by the sound of a car door closing and almost at once the kitchen filled with women. He took a grocery sack that was threatening to fall out his mother's arms and put it on the counter.

Mandy flew threw the door right behind her followed by a chuckling Caroline.

Amid a flurry of chatter they managed to get the cars unloaded. A few minutes later they were again enjoying coffee around the table when Everett Lynch walked in. "I stopped at the Pizza Hut. Almost let the car take me into KFC but remembered we had that last time."

He unloaded pizza boxes on the counter and bent over to kiss his wife. Gabe watched Taylor out of the corner of his eye. She looked almost mesmerized by the noise and family interaction and it didn't look like a hello kiss was something she saw much of. Or, that she'd had much experience in participating in. *Now where had that come from?*

Mandy had one thing on her mind and it wasn't dinner, even when there was pizza. "Can I put on my new princess pajamas?" She turned toward Gabe. "Taylor brought them for me."

Gabe feigned surprise. "Pajamas!" He pointed to the clock on the wall. "At this time of day?"

Mandy's lower lip jutted out. "But, I'm tired, Daddy. Really, really tired." She faked a yawn.

He winked at Taylor to let her know he was playing. "But little girls need a bath before they get into their pajamas and they have to eat dinner and . . ."

Mandy cocked her head and Gabe waited as her six year old mind battled with her stomach. The stomach won and she slid onto a chair. "Okay, but let's get this show on the road."

Lillian, Caroline's mother, couldn't hold back her laughter. "I'm sorry, Gabe." She choked. Turning away she got up to get dishes out for the pizza. "Will paper plates be okay?"

A chorus of yes, and you betcha's sounded off as Eric, Caroline's husband-to-be, walked in the door. "What did I miss? Whatever, I'm voting with Gabe 'cuz he's the biggest."

Caroline walked over, and gave him a hug. "Yeah but I'm the toughest."

Gabe winked and added, "She isn't kidding either. I

remember the time she . . ."

Caroline put her hand over his mouth, cutting off the sentence. "Don't you dare. Remember, I can tell some juicy stories about you too."

He held up his hands. "I give." Looking over at Eric he said, "See I wouldn't mess around with her."

* * * * *

Taylor felt like she had entered an alternate world. First, dinner at four thirty? Her father would have termed anything before eight as barbaric. Then the horseplay and teasing. She swallowed a lump in her throat, excused herself and ran upstairs.

Why did it hurt so much to feel what she knew, what she'd always known. No man would walk into a room and have eyes for only her like Mr. Lynch did for his wife or like Eric had for Caroline. People envied her, for her wealth, for her looks, for the opulence she lived in but in her world people didn't sit around a table joking and just enjoying each other's company.

She rinsed her face and patted it dry. The bathroom connected to the bedroom she was using so thankfully she had makeup handy to do repairs.

She opened the door and stopped short. Gabe was leaning against the wall.

"You okay?"

"Sure, you didn't have to . . ."

"I know, but you looked a little pale when you left the kitchen."

A warm glow filled her at his concern. She smiled her thank you at him. When he motioned for her to go ahead of him she felt his eyes follow her and the heat level of the glow ratcheted up a couple of levels.

6

Caught up in wedding talk, no one said anything when
Gabe and Taylor walked back into the kitchen together.
Gabe took a couple of sodas out of the fridge and handed
one to her.

Instead of pouring the soda into a glass, he handed her
the can. Again that warm glow spread over her. No one
treated her as if she was different and it felt good.

Talk flowed around the table until Gabe's beeper went
off. Mumbling he had to take it, he left the table.

Caroline started picking up plates and Eric pulled out
the garbage can from under the sink. "Whew, guess if we're
going to get anything done at the house tonight we'd better
get going."

Caroline had told Taylor all about the house that they
had purchased, and that Eric was sort of camping out in it
while they did some painting. They had moved out of the

apartment last weekend to sleep apart until the wedding.

Caroline's mother took over, and told them to go. "Dad and I'll have this little bit cleaned up in a jiff."

"Thanks mom. Come on Taylor. We'll put you to work."

Taylor started to answer but stopped as Gabe came through the door. "I've got to take this call and it's clear out at Red Creek."

His mother nodded. "Mandy's okay here for the night or would you rather I take her home and put her to bed?"

"Whatever is easier for you. Text me what you decide." Mandy had been quietly playing with her wand and Barbie dolls and Gabe reached down to give her a kiss on the top of her head. "Be a good girl for Grammy. Love you Bumpkin."

With a wave at everyone and a quick glance her way, he left the room. Taylor was surprised he'd filled so much of it that it felt empty. She looked over at Caroline. "You two go ahead. I'll stay here and help Lillian."

"You sure?" Caroline didn't look like she felt comfortable leaving her. But Eric had to work the next day and Taylor could tell he appreciated some alone time with Caroline tonight. At his wink she mentally added another point to her list. And, another vibe that she really did fit in.

She laughed. "Tell you what, tomorrow I'll go over there with you and maybe we can surprise Eric with what we get done."

After everyone left and the kitchen was put back in order, Mr. and Mrs. Lynch moved into the family room adjoining the kitchen and turned on the TV. Taylor started to join them, but hesitated when Mandy stayed at the table with her toys.

"She's fine dear. Come watch Wheel of Fortune with us."

"Then can I take a bath and put my new pajamas on?" Mandy's voice held anticipation.

Taylor didn't wait for Lillian's reply. "I could take Mandy home and stay with her until Gabe gets back."

Mandy looked like she was holding her breath and about ready to burst while they waited for her grandmother's response.

"Oh, that would be wonderful but are you sure? We don't want to impose. It's just that it being Saturday tomorrow, the clinic is only open until noon. Gabe likes to have breakfast with Mandy and then take her in with him on these short days."

Taylor squeezed the little hand that had slipped into hers. "I'm positive and it won't be any imposition at all."

Mandy had her coat on and the gift bag Taylor had brought and was back downstairs in record time. "I'm ready when you are," she chirped.

Everett held out his arms. "In so much of a hurry you can't spare a goodbye hug for Grandpa."

Mandy flew across the room to hug both her grandparents and then rushed back beside Taylor. "Come on. I'll show you my room and we can watch a movie after I get my pajamas on and . . ."

Taylor slipped on her own coat, and waved goodbye to a smiling set of grandparents.

Mandy took her hand. "We live at the end of the driveway. It's not very far."

Taylor gave the little hand another squeeze. The night was cold and clear. She was surprised at how many stars lit up the sky. It reminded her of the sky over the French convent where she'd gone to elementary school. Memories of that time flooded over her. For awhile she'd considered joining the convent but, like Manhattan, she'd never really felt like she belonged. Did she belong anywhere, or was she destined to always be on the outside looking in? She thought about what her father had asked of her. Would marriage to her father's protégé be an answer? She would have her own home. Her father had told her he would purchase the penthouse apartment in the sister building to his for a wedding present, and that he would make Frederick a full partner. Mandy pulled on her hand breaking into her thoughts.

Taylor frowned when Mandy ran up on the back porch and swung the door open. Didn't Gabe lock the door? She'd never heard of anyone not locking their door.

They entered a large room with a washer, dryer and bench. Mandy sat down and pulled off her shoes. She looked up at Taylor and said, "You don't have to take your shoes off. Grownups don't . . ."

"No, I'll take mine off and then we'll both be in our stockings."

Mandy laughed at this and whispered, "Then we can both jump on my bed."

Taylor's laugh rang out and mingled with the little girl's.

The house was new if the stainless steel appliances wood floors and granite counter tops were any indication. It was spotlessly clean and beautiful but missed the warmth and lived-in feel of the family home they had just left.

Mandy was chattering a mile a minute which seemed to be her normal mode and seemed to easily transition between the two places.

Taylor followed Mandy through the kitchen to the front of the house and upstairs to her room. Curious, Taylor noted that most of the rooms weren't furnished. The dining room and formal living room didn't have any furniture. It looked like Gabe and Mandy lived in the kitchen which had a family area with a fireplace.

The staircase had a landing half way up. Good for small children that might fall the full length of a straight one. Had Mandy been a baby in this house?

At the top of the stairs Mandy glanced over her shoulder and Taylor winked reassuring her she was right behind her. She turned left at the head of the stairs and said, "Daddy's room is that way." She pointed to the right. Her little face took on a serious look. "When he sleeps in it. Most of the time he sleeps on the couch."

Whoops, bet that was more than she was supposed to know. Oh well, wait until he discovered she had heard his conversation in the café. Where he slept would pale in comparison.

Taylor was half asleep when she heard Gabe come in. Amanda had begged her to stay in her room and Taylor had given in. The door creaked and light from the hall fell across the bed. She feigned sleep. She wasn't sure he shared the attraction she was feeling but better to be safe. Late at night, alone with only a sleeping child to diffuse the situation, it would be wise to avoid going there. She felt the bed shift when he leaned over and tucked the covers around Mandy. Then she felt the warmth of a blanket as he gently spread it over her. The blanket felt good. The caring felt better.

She listened as he left the room, she'd just lie here until she was sure he was asleep before getting up and going back to his parent's place.

* * * * *

A branch scratched across the window and Taylor slowly opened her eyes. Mandy was still asleep and it felt like it was early. Good, she eased out of bed and folded the blanket. Quietly she made her way down the stairs and into the kitchen where she stopped short. Gabe sat at the bar holding a steaming cup of coffee. His gaze locked with hers.

Taylor swallowed. Things, feelings, everything was strange and new. Yet they also felt right somehow. Like she was meant to be in this time and place. Like the man in front of her was . . . She blinked, breaking eye contact. "I didn't know anyone was up."

"Barely, grab a cup." His voice sounded deep in the quiet room. He ran a hand through his hair adding to the just-got-up look. With morning whiskers, bare feet and a T-shirt molded over abs that looked like they belonged on a model, he looked like something Taylor had only seen in the movies or maybe, if she were honest, in her dreams. She bit back a groan; she was truly out of her element.

"I should get back up to the house. Your mother will be up and wondering what happened to me."

He shook his head. "My mother isn't an early riser, and they know where you are. You have time for a cup of coffee. What kind of a host would I be if I sent you back without even that?"

His look said more and Taylor felt warmth flood her cheeks. "Here, sit down and I'll get you a cup."

"No, stay still, I'll get it." She filled her cup and topped his off, then leaned against the bar on the kitchen side.

Gabe took a drink of coffee and said, "I didn't expect to find you here this morning."

Taking a swallow from her own cup she again met his eyes. "You knew I wasn't sleeping last night."

"I figured you were planning to wait until I went to my room and then leave."

"I fell asleep."

He smiled and Taylor caught her breath when her heart picked up its beat. Relief flooded over her when he didn't pursue it. Instead he said, "So how did it go with Mandy? She's pretty taken with you."

Taylor felt herself relax. "I'm pretty taken with her. Caroline writes lots of Mandy stories and I've gotten to know and love her. But I wasn't prepared for what a fantastic little girl she is in real life."

"She is."

Again silence fell over the room. And something else, something Taylor hadn't experienced. Excitement, yearning, awareness of not only Gabe but of herself. She tamped down what she was feeling and turned to put her cup in the sink. "I really need to get going. Your mother and Caroline have a lot planned for today."

"Stay."

Taylor felt his voice as much as she heard it. Her skin tingled. She caught her breath at the sensation of it flowing over her. She wanted to stay, she wanted . . .

"We'll fix breakfast for Mandy and I'll walk you up to the house." His eyes skimmed over her face and rested on her mouth.

Taylor glanced at the clock, seven o'clock, ten Manhattan time. "How long will Mandy sleep?"

Gabe stood up and motioned toward the family room where the fireplace was going. "Another hour, maybe two. Grab another cup of coffee. This will be a good time for us to get better acquainted. Caroline has sung your praises so much and so often we all feel like we know you."

She smiled, she knew exactly how he felt. "Okay, I'd like that. You have an amazing daughter, an amazing family."

Out of the blue he said, "And you heard the conversation in the café the other day."

It wasn't a question and the statement was so unexpected, it caught her by surprise. "Wow, I didn't see that coming."

Gabe chuckled and the mood lightened. If this was his way of breaking the ice, he'd done it in spades.

"Sorry, but seeing you when I walked into Mom and Dad's yesterday was a bit of shock. So . . ."

She followed him across the room and took the end of the sofa. He passed up the chair and took the other end. Leaning back he put his feet up on the coffee table and rested his cup on his lap. He looked like a man comfortable with himself; she'd never seen her father or any other guy like this. What about Frederick? Taylor frowned. She couldn't picture Frederick in anything but a designer suit, complete with name brand shoes. And, he wouldn't have a scent like Gabe's. Like fresh air and . . . man.

She pulled her thoughts back. "It sounded like your friend was trying to play matchmaker. Something about Internet dating?" Again a warmth spread over her face. She ducked her head. "I'm sorry. I would never have brought it up if you . . ."

"I know, I did. For me it was fast becoming an elephant in the room. Anyway you have to admit the topic is an ice breaker."

They both burst out laughing. It was all of that. Taylor leaned over, and put her cup on the table. She hadn't combed her hair, she had rinsed out her mouth and used a washcloth for a makeshift toothbrush. Her mother and father would be . . . what? Surprised? Probably more like appalled. In their home breakfast was served and even in casual morning wear they were fully groomed.

Gabe's eyes crinkled with laugh lines. "It's okay you know. You can let go and be yourself. I don't know how things work in New York but here we pretty much say what's on our mind. We laugh a lot as you can see." His voice dropped lower, as if a memory had walked across his mind.

"It is different, but thanks to Caroline it also feels familiar." She felt mischievous, an unfamiliar emotion, as she turned the tables on him again and said, "So, are you going to run an ad? I can help you write it if you'd like."

This time his laugh rang out. "Oh, you think so huh, and what would you say?"

Taylor put her finger on her chin in a mockery of thinking. "Well I could say . . . No, better not say that. Let's see maybe . . . No not that."

She held up her hands. "Guess I'll need some time to think about this. After all you want to catch . . ."

A sound from the stairs stopped their verbal play. Mandy's eyes widened when she saw Taylor and a smile lit up her face. So much for another one or two hours sleep.

Taylor held out her arms to the little girl. She glanced over at Gabe and saw the love in his eyes as he watched them. And, something else, something that looked like yearning.

7

Gabe couldn't keep his eyes off Taylor. Yesterday, even though she'd just woken up from a nap, she had been perfectly groomed. She wore her hair in a severe pulled back style. If she had glasses she could have been cast as a librarian. This morning was a new picture; her hair softly curled around her face and fell just below her shoulders. She was so close the scent of it washed over him.

Mandy's voice broke the spell. "Daddy, I don't want eggs. I want cereal."

"You like scrambled eggs with bacon."

Her little face took on a serious look. "Not this morning."

Gabe laughed. "Okay, cereal it is. Taylor and I will eat this good stuff."

The little girl looked over at where Taylor had popped bread into the toaster. "I'll have a piece of Taylor's toast with my cereal."

Taylor winked at him and his heart raced pumping blood through his body and parts best not to think about.

Mandy set the table, chattering away as she carefully folded a napkin for each of them. She was a great little chaperone, not letting Taylor out of her sight. Gabe felt a pang of regret as he realized again that the presence of a mother was missing in his daughter's life. Why hadn't he realized how bad Mandy wanted a family? In closing himself off from a relationship he was also depriving his daughter.

They were just sitting down at the table when Caroline walked in. "Brr, its cold out there." She walked over, and grabbed a cup from the cupboard.

Gabe motioned toward the stove. "Grab a plate, I made plenty. Especially since our little princess wants cereal."

Taylor watched as Caroline helped herself. "I'm sorry I didn't make it back to your parent's house last night. I fell asleep with Mandy. As soon as I finish this great breakfast that your brother made, I'll be ready to help you and your mother."

Caroline dismissed Taylor's concern. "No need to hurry. Mom sort of has her own routine. In fact she shooed me out." She turned toward Gabe. "When are you going to cut the evergreens and fall foliage for me?"

"I thought I'd take a run up to Copper Creek this afternoon. Mandy has a birthday party/sleep over so as soon as I drop her off I'll cut out. Do you want to go?"

"I'd like to." Caroline looked over at Taylor. "I'm using the fall leaves on the vine maples and cedar boughs in the floral decorations."

Caroline had chosen to keep her wedding small. She had only two attendants. Taylor's dress was a rich copper, with a simple elegant cut.

"It will be beautiful. Are you going to do the arrangements yourself or hire a florist?"

"I'm going to do them."

"I can help you with the easy part if you tell me what to do."

"That's great, I'm not going to do anything fancy. I appreciate your help. We got behind when it took the purchase of the house so long to close." Turning back to Gabe, Caroline added, "Guess that answers your question. I'd love to get out in the fresh air but I really need to get moved into the house."

Taylor had been to a lot of events and in charge of a few. Weddings, fund raisers, parties, but all of them had been catered and professionally arranged. This was the first time she'd been on the doing end of things. It might be exhausting for Caroline but she caught the air of excitement from her friend. "So what exactly do you have planned for the day and how can I help?"

"Eric thought he had to work, but got an unexpected day off. We thought we had better run up to his parents place. They live about an hour southeast of here. We hope to get back early enough to move the furniture into the bedrooms."

Taylor took a drink of her coffee and got up to put her dishes and cup in the dishwasher. Gabe stood and took them from her. "Here, I'll get that."

She didn't turn loose, and for a minute they both hung onto the plate. Smiling he gently tugged and she let it go. A current passed between them and Taylor stepped back. Had Caroline seen it, felt it?

Taylor turned toward the door. "If Gabe isn't going to let me help clean up I'll get my coat and we can get out of his way so he can get ready for work."

"No hurry, all I have to do is walk the few feet to the clinic." He picked up Mandy's bowl and motioned her toward the stairs. "Go get dressed, just jeans for now. You'll have time to change before the party."

Caroline said, "What time is her party?"

"Two, they are going to a movie, then the pizza place for dinner, then a sleep over."

Caroline smiled at Mandy. "Wow, you are going to have quite a weekend."

"Yep, I bought Susie a Halloween Barbie and I'm going to take my new pajamas. I only wore them one night and I was careful not to get my cereal on them."

Caroline hugged her and said, "So I see."

Gabe again told his daughter to get dressed. This time, she moved. He turned back to Caroline and Taylor. "I'll take off straight from dropping Mandy off and head up the canyon to get your leaves and cedar."

He walked them to the door and held Taylor's coat for her. When she felt his hands on the collar, she pulled her hair up out of the way and fought the urge to lean back into him. How many men had helped her with her coat? Yet, never had she felt the warm flush of arousal like this. If Caroline weren't here she wasn't sure she would have had the strength to pull away.

Caroline seemed oblivious to what was going on behind her. Taylor turned to follow her but Gabe's hand found hers. His voice was a soft whisper. "Come with me."

Taylor looked up and met his gaze. "I . . . can't. Caroline needs me to help with the wedding." She realized she was whispering back and drew in a breath. In a normal voice, she said, "I can't."

Caroline asked, "Can't what?"

Gabe squeezed Taylor's hand again before he let it go. "I just asked your friend to come with me to collect the foliage you need. And, . . ."

"And, I said I couldn't. I came a few days early to help you."

Caroline shook her head. "But that will be perfect. Nothing personal brother dear, but a woman's eye will make certain I get the foliage I need. All Eric and I are doing is taking some things down to his dad so he can sell them for us. We don't plan on staying long so by the time you guys get done we should be back and you can come over and help us move the furniture."

Taylor wasn't convinced and her face must have shown it because Caroline followed up with, "Besides it will give Mom and Dad a break. Mom has been so busy and with family coming for the wedding she's going to be even busier this coming week. Maybe with all of us out of the house she'll take a nap."

Taylor threw up her hands. "You guys, let's run it by your mother and see what she says."

Gabe leaned in close and whispered. "See you this

afternoon Princess."

She glanced back to see a gleam in his eyes that said he knew his mother. A tingle started in her chest and fluttered down her body as excitement raced through her. She hoped he was right.

8

Taylor smiled as Mandy lugged her overnight bag down the porch stairs. She made quite a production out of it, and gave an exaggerated sigh when she slammed the back door of the truck.

As suspected Gabe's mother encouraged her to go with him to pick the fall foliage. When he had called to tell her he'd pick her up, she told him she'd walk down and now was glad that she had, because she would have hated to miss the Mandy dramatics.

Gabe came out of the house chuckling. "Caught the act huh? I offered to take her bag but . . ."

Mandy interrupted him. "Daddy! I'm a big girl now."

"So you are, but ladies let the guys help them. Right, Taylor?" His eyes twinkled and his wink made her heart skip a beat.

He opened the door and reached in to shift Mandy's

overnight bag over, then turned and lifted the little girl in. "Want some help with the seatbelt bumpkin?"

"Yes, please."

Taylor reached for the passenger door but Gabe reached around, and covered her hand with his. "Let a guy help." His lips were close to her ear and his voice resonated, deep and rich. She fought the urge to close her eyes. Seconds spun out until Mandy's little voice piped up to tell them she was ready to go.

"Later." Gabe whispered.

Taylor watched as Gabe backed the truck out of the drive. The day was unusually warm for late October and Gabe pushed the sleeves of his sweatshirt up showing strong forearms. She pulled her gaze away and watched the countryside slide by. Two days, and yet it felt like a lifetime. This morning while she waited for Gabe, she had helped clean the spare bedrooms and change linens. A new experience for her because at home she never made her bed let alone put on clean sheets. And dusting and vacuuming?

"Are we almost there yet Daddy?"

Gabe rolled his eyes at Taylor and answered. "You know better. Look out the window and tell me when to turn."

"Okay." Came back the little voice.

Gabe laughed. "I've promised her a Disneyland trip but I don't think it's going to be a road trip."

"Disneyland sounds like fun."

"Have you been there?" He asked.

"No." The tone of her voice surprised her. It was like

there was another conversation going on between them.

It wasn't far to Mandy's friends' house, probably a good thing because the little girl was so excited she could hardly contain herself. Gabe pulled up in front of the rambler and walked Mandy to the door. He talked to the lady who came out to greet them and was chuckling when he got back in the truck. "Whew, from the sounds I could hear, there's a lot of energy in that house. Not sure I'm up for it when Mandy's turn comes to be the birthday girl."

"You'll manage, by the time she graduates . . ."

He held up his hand. "Don't go there; she's only in the first grade." His voice grew serious. "But time is already moving too fast. Sometimes it feels like she's six going on sixteen."

Gabe reached over, and took her hand. Taylor looked down and a tingle moved over her at the sight of their joined hands.

Silence filled the truck and Taylor breathed in Gabe's scent. Unlike the smell of expensive cologne her father and Frederick used, Gabe's scent was a clean, fresh air smell with a warm masculine under-laying aroma. His voice broke the silence. "Tell me about yourself. Caroline said you work in your father's firm? Is there anyone special waiting for you?"

"No, yes." Gabe's question took Taylor by surprise. Was she in a relationship? He waited for her to say more. She took a deep breath. "There is someone but I guess I don't think of Frederick as special. I've known him for ten years and my father expects us to marry. He wants to announce the engagement when I get back."

"What do you want? What does Frederick want? Arranged marriages are archaic to say the least."

Taylor pulled her hand away. How did she explain her world to Gabe? How did she explain that in her world you did what Father wanted? And Father wanted anything that benefitted his firm. Her whole life had been in pleasing him. So how did she explain when she wasn't sure she understood herself? She didn't love Frederick but she liked him. He treated her like a . . . porcelain princess. When he needed her looks, or her name, he escorted her on his arm and there was the matter of him making partner. Marrying him would be a win, win for them both. It would allow her to work at the free legal clinic without the hassle she got from her father. Frederick didn't like her to talk about her work downtown, but he looked the other way. *Or least he does now*, a niggling voice in her head said.

Taylor couldn't look at Gabe. Instead she stared out the front window. "I work in my father's firm. Frederick is up for partner. We have a lot in common it would be a good marriage."

Gabe pulled the truck over at a view point. His voice seemed to caress her. "Look at me."

Taylor swallowed the lump in her throat. She shook her head. Why had she agreed to come with him? He made her question her life in ways she didn't understand.

Gabe again said, "Look at me. Tell me I'm out of line. Tell me that you're not feeling the current flowing between us. Tell me you don't want me to kiss you." His voice dropped. "I feel so alive with you."

Taylor wasn't sure if she moved to him first, but the

next second she was in his arms and his mouth was teasing hers open. She didn't think, instead she let her senses take over, and pressed against his hard chest. A moan escaped him. When she felt his hand move to her breast, she shifted to give him better access. No one had ever touched her like this. His mouth moved down her throat and she tilted her head back. Her breast ached for more. She couldn't believe the sounds coming from her as they mingled with his.

A car roared past, barely registering with Taylor until Gabe drew back. His breathing made his voice sound ragged. "We need to get off this main road. The turn off to the ridge is just a little bit farther."

Taylor didn't trust her voice and instead nodded.

"Scoot over here by me. There's a middle seat belt here someplace." Gabe found it and helped her fasten it. He again took her hand and this time kissed the palm before pressing it against his leg.

When silence filled the truck it felt warm and rich. Excitement coursed through her making her want to touch Gabe in ways that made her blush. He wore his hair longer than the styles worn by the men she knew and she liked it. He took his eyes off the road and his gaze filled hers. She could see what she felt reflected in them and another current of need filled her.

"The place I am going to cut the branches is secluded. Stay with me, we'll be there in a few minutes."

Taylor was surprised at the tremor in her voice. "This probably isn't a good idea. I mean what will your family think."

"Honey, I'm thirty five years old, if they think anything

at all it will probably be to say it's about time." He squeezed her hand and brought it up to his mouth to press heated kisses across her palm.

Her lips formed an O when she felt moist pressure between her legs.

He was in perfect tune with her and whispered. "Stay with it, stay with me, honey. I'm feeling it with you."

How did he know? It felt like they were of one mind. What would it feel like to be of one body?

* * * * *

Gabe gripped the wheel with both hands. He had to let go of Taylor's hand when they got to the logging road but she kept it on his leg. He didn't know what was happening, nothing he'd planned. Hell, in his wildest dreams he wouldn't have conjured up what was happening to him and, unless he was off, the beautiful woman sitting so close to him was feeling the same way. Finally, he saw the fork in the road he was looking for and a few minutes later he pulled under a big cedar and parked the truck. When he turned he met Taylor's eyes. Like his, they spoke of need and want. He unbuckled his seat belt and reached around her to get hers. There was no awkwardness when he pulled her into his arms. She opened her mouth and mated it with his. He wasn't sure how experienced she was, and before he went further he'd damn well better find out. Some of the things she'd said, some of the things Caroline had said, made him think she might not have dated much. He pulled her closer. She felt so good. He ran his hand under her sweater feeling the softness of her skin. She arched her back giving him access and his heart rate picked up speed.

Her eyes were closed and her breathing was as labored as his. It had been so long, but what he was feeling wasn't due to his self imposed abstinence. It was more like finding a part of himself he hadn't known existed. He tilted her head up with his hands. "Look at me. Are you sure?"

Slowly her eyes opened and she met his gaze. The tip of her tongue wet her lips and he heard a groan erupt from his chest. Again he asked, "Honey, are you sure?"

"No."

Pain laced through his groin. "No?"

She held his gaze and he marveled at the passion that was in her eyes. It equaled his own.

"I'm not sure; but what I am sure of is that I don't want to stop."

The day was unseasonably warm. Gabe reached over the seat and grabbed a blanket, grateful for it and the weather. He opened his door and stepped out holding his hand for Taylor to take. When she did he lifted her out and let her slide down his body. She melted into him and lifted her mouth to his. When he felt her tongue play across his lips he deepened the kiss. This wasn't the act of an inexperienced woman. He buried his mouth in her neck and again moved his hands under her sweater. Fighting for control he motioned toward an overgrown trail. "There's a sheltered place by the river."

She nodded and took his hand until the narrow trail forced her to step ahead. Gabe watched the swing of her hips and drew in a sharp breath. He didn't remember ever being this hard, this ready.

Taylor stopped at the edge of the clearing. "Oh Gabe,

this is beautiful."

He smiled and stepped up beside her. "I'm glad you like it." He spread the blanket out and sat down, pulling her over the top of him to cushion her from the hard ground.

His eyes sought hers. "I know this is too soon but we have so little time."

She put her fingers over his lips then leaned down and kissed him. He could feel the softness of her breasts and shifted so their bodies made full contact. He ran his hands under her sweater and unclasped her bra. "Are you too cold to take off some clothes?"

She laughed. "Somehow I don't think the temperature is going to be a problem."

"Somehow I think you are right."

She lifted her arms and he pulled the bra and sweater off in one motion. "My god, you're beautiful." He pulled her mouth back to his and hunger took over. He sensed the same hunger in her and it was all he could do to sit up to get his own shirt off.

Leaning over her he said, "Now where were we?"

For an answer she pushed him away and reached for his belt buckle. They both rose up on their knees and Gabe again took Taylor's mouth.

Breathing hard they helped each other out of their clothes. "Tell me if I'm going too fast." He whispered.

For an answer she ran her hands down to his waist, then to his hips. He bucked forward letting her feel his erection. Surely she was experienced, but he needed to slow down. If she had regrets it was going to kill him.

When her hand ran up the length of his arousal he

sucked in his breath and any idea of going slow fled his mind. Still he paused, his eyes silently questioned her. Then he gently laid her back on the blanket.

When she closed her eyes he whispered. "Look at me. I want to know you to have no doubts, no regrets and I want to look into your eyes when I claim you.

She went still, and fear raced through him. Had his words scared her?

Taylor ran her hands up the back of his neck into his hair and arched her hips for penetration. "Put your legs around my waist." He ground out.

Taking it as slow as his body would let him he eased into her. She circled his hips with her legs.

She was tight, a new rush of desire rushed through him. When he met her body's natural resistance, he stopped and pulled back.

Her gaze still held his. "Don't stop, please don't stop."

As if he could. "I . . . I don't want . . ."

"I do." She tightened her legs and pushed up taking the decision from him.

He willed himself to wait for her body to adjust to his size, then slowly moved in a dance as old as time.

He felt like he was about to burst and fought for control. He wanted her, no he needed for her to climax with him. When he felt her contract around him, he wanted to shout to the heavens and followed her over the edge in a dual free-fall of pleasure.

He lifted up with his forearms to take his weight off her and listened as her breathing slowed with his. Still joined, he nuzzled her neck, taking her on a journey of foreplay they had bypassed.

He hardened inside her again and she pressed closer. He caught his breath and withdrew to discard the protection he had managed to put on. His deep voice whispered. "It isn't safe, we should stop. You'll be sore, the first time . . ."

She reached up and ran her hand over his bare back. "It's a good sore, more like awareness." She smiled. "I like it."

His chuckle came from deep in his chest. Her nipples hardened and she rubbed against his arm.

Gabe quickly sheathed himself. "Come here."

He tried to pace himself, to make it last. She was unbelievably responsive; when he felt her second orgasm he again claimed her mouth and let himself go.

Gabe rolled over on his back and waited for his breathing to slow. He felt ten feet tall, like shouting, like . . . When he could finally speak he whispered. "Say this isn't a dream."

"If this is a dream, I don't want to wake up. I never knew . . ."

He kissed her neck and felt her heart speed up. His voice breathed against her heated skin. "Why didn't you tell me?"

"When?" She hid her face against his chest. "We were a bit busy. Plus I'd hoped you wouldn't know, wouldn't think that I was inexperienced."

He lifted her chin to see her face. Was she teasing him? "I could have hurt you. Or not satisfied you. The first time, especially if the membrane is intact can be painful." He traced his finger over lips swollen with his possession. Thankfully none of what he was telling her had happened.

A peach colored blush stole over her face, and he marveled at the beauty of it. He'd never encountered passion like hers. If time could stop he would want it to stop here, to spend the rest of his live nestled against her in a secluded woodland setting. With regret he leaned in to give her a light kiss but at the first touch, he deepened it and felt himself again harden. Unbelievable, physics dictated that a man needed to recover, though being with Taylor, rendered those laws a myth. Empowered, he pulled her closer.

A cool breeze brought him back to his senses and he moved away from her. "It feels like the temperature is dropping. As bad as I hate it, we need to get dressed and get out of the woods.

He handed her clothes to her and reached for his own. Getting to his feet, he held his hand down for her. "Are you okay?"

She smiled and he relaxed, their love making had been fantastic for him and he wanted it to be the same for her but he didn't want to ask the mundane question of *was it as good for you as it was for me.*

"I'm fine, better than fine. But . . ."

"But?" He moved back to her and dipped his head for a kiss. "I can't get enough of you. I want to touch, to taste, oh honey don't let there be any buts."

Her eyes held his. "What about Caroline? What about your parents? I'm a guest in their home. What will they think of what I've done?"

Gabe glanced at the sky as another cooler blast of air

forewarned of a deeper chill on the way. They needed to collect the branches and get on the road. Weather this time of year could be unpredictable, especially with nightfall. "First of all it wasn't what you did. It is what we did and what we did is natural, and beautiful, and it's ours. All they need to know is we're happy, and that will make them happy."

He wasn't sure she was reassured, today had to have been a huge step for her and he felt humbled that she trusted him. Excitement coursed through him. He had so much to teach her about love. *Love! He hadn't seen that coming.*

9

Gabe silently thanked the fates for his decision to get a bench seat in the truck as he helped Taylor in from the driver's side. He got in behind her, and leaned in for a kiss. He wanted more but it was getting late and cold. "You taste so good, it's a wonder we got the leaves and branches collected."

Taylor's eyes were bright, she looked happy." We have a lot. Do you think Caroline will need this much?"

"Better to be safe. If she has some left over I can use them to decorate the clinic and Mom will always take some. There might even be enough to decorate my house. I've never done it before. Mandy and I usually just enjoy the holiday stuff at Mom and Dad's."

"Mandy will love it. Maybe if there isn't enough we could bring her back up here to collect more."

"I like the sound of 'we'. I could get used to having you in my life."

He rested his arm over the seat and maneuvered the truck out to the trail as renewed awareness of Taylor shot through him. Her scent teased his senses. He wanted to stop the truck and . . . Clenching his jaw he reminded himself it was getting late.

Taylor rested her hand on Gabe's leg without being prompted and he covered it with his. He smiled and said, "I don't want to go over to Caroline and Eric's tonight. How do you feel about taking a rain check?"

Taylor took her time answering. "She will be disappointed."

His voice deepened. "What about you? Will you be disappointed?"

He felt her eyes on him and glanced over. How was it possible that she could become more beautiful with each minute he was with her?

She pulled her hand from under his and turned his over. When she rubbed her thumb over his palm, he bit back a moan. Damn, he didn't want to share her with anyone tonight.

Her voice sounded soft in the darkening cab. "I came to help Caroline, I won't be much of a friend if I . . ."

He squeezed her hand. "You're right. I know I'm being selfish." His voice took on a teasing tone. "But maybe she'll be tired. I'll call her when we get down far enough for a signal."

They rode in silence for a few miles. Gabe's thoughts were on 'what next?' He wanted to ask her to stay the night with him. Mandy wouldn't be home, but what about the next night. If they spent one night together, would Taylor share his concerns for diplomacy when Mandy was with him? He knew so little about her. Taking a breath he said, "Tell me a little more about yourself? How much time do you spend on pro bono work?"

She looked over at him but didn't say anything. Silence again filled the cab. He glanced over at her and smiled, encouraging her to open up to him.

"Not as much as I'd like. Hamilton & Associates is a demanding firm, even more so when you're the bosses' daughter." She drew in a deep breath and said, "If this is a getting to know you conversation it's your turn. How long has it been since you were in a relationship?"

"Wow, you get right to the heart of it." She had taken her hand off his leg and he took it back, before answering. "I guess it's only fair, you told me about Frederick." He paused for a second then said, "I haven't been with anyone since Bonnie."

Taylor looked like she didn't know what to say. He thought that Caroline would have written her about the accident that claimed his wife but maybe not. "That was almost three years ago. Sometimes it seems like yesterday. Maybe I'm just getting older because I can remember when it seemed like a lifetime between Christmases."

Taylor smiled, his reference to Christmas seemed to lighten the mood in the cab. "You're right; the older we get the more it seems there is never enough time."

The mood lasted for only a few seconds. Something was bothering her. "Go ahead, you can ask me anything."

"No, it's okay."

He picked up her hand and kissed her fingers. His voice resonated through the truck, deep and rich. "What do you want to ask me?"

Taylor pulled her hand away. "It's just that you were so . . ."

"So what? Come on honey, you are scaring me." His heart rate picked up. Did she have regrets about making love? Granted it wasn't the best scenario for a first time but it had been impossibly beautiful for him. He waited, willing her to not say she was sorry they'd made love.

"It's just that you . . . do you always carry protection?"

The last words almost exploded out of her. Relief washed over him and he bit back a chuckle. "No, once upon a time I wouldn't have left home without them but that hasn't been the case for years." He swallowed. "I didn't even have any in the house, Pete came into the clinic this morning and I sent him down to get me some."

Taylor gasped out. "You did what? Oh my gosh, did he know I was going to go with you today?" She closed her eyes. "I can't believe you did that. He will know what we did."

Gabe laughed and she socked him on the shoulder. "Don't you dare laugh. This isn't funny. I won't be able to face him at the wedding."

Still laughing, he pulled the truck over to the side of the road and tried to take her in his arms but she smacked him on the chest.

"Come on honey, one look at my face and Pete would know even if he hadn't run that errand for me."

Taylor hugged herself and moaned. "I can't believe this."

Gabe unbuckled his seat belt and reached over to undo hers. He took Taylor's hands down from her head and held them in one of his. With his other hand he tilted her chin up. "Look at me."

He almost gasped at the look in her eyes. What had he done? He was close with Pete, they had shared almost everything for most of their lives. They drew the line at kissing and telling but getting a box of condoms? He hadn't given it a thought. Until now.

"Listen to me honey; doing that errand is as far as it goes." He moved back and ran his hands through his hair. "What happened today was something natural. It was beautiful and, well, right. Having people see us as a couple makes me . . . hell it makes me feel ten feet tall." He paused to get control of his voice. "The only thing I'm sorry for is if it's an embarrassment for you."

This time when he reached for her Taylor came into his arms. His voice sounded husky in the confines of the cab. "I don't want you to have any regrets. This wasn't sex for me. It was more, so much more that I'm still reeling from it."

Her words were muffled against his neck. "It can't go any further than this Gabe. We live a continent away and worlds apart."

He knew this, had known it from the first time he'd seen her and felt the undeniable pull of attraction. So why the gut wrenching feeling of loss at her words? Making the decision to live for the moment he said, "Let's not think about that now. We have the rest of the week. And, if you don't have to go back right away, maybe another few days after the wedding." He kissed the top of her head and moved away to restart the truck. It was time to get back on the road.

The sun was setting as they drove off the logging road and reached a point where they could call Caroline. Her voice sounded cheerful over the phone's speaker. Taylor couldn't wait for her to see the beautiful vine maple leaves they'd collected. "Are you home?"

"Yes, we got back later than we had hoped. About forty five minutes ago. Where are you guys?"

Taylor looked over at Gabe. She had no idea where they were. He winked at her and said, "Hi sis, we are about half an hour or so from home. What do you want to do with this forest in the back of my truck?"

Caroline chuckled and said, "Can you meet us at Mom and Dad's? Eric has to be in an early morning meeting in Seattle tomorrow and wants to drive over tonight. We can unload the foliage and then run out for a bite to eat before he leaves."

Gabe responded. "Sure, can do, see you in a few." He started to push the button on his steering wheel. Blue Tooth technology was great, no trouble to talk hands free with it.

He paused as Caroline said, "Wait, Taylor? I thought we could stay here at the house tonight. It will just be you and me. We could get the rest of the things put away and be all moved in. What do you think?"

Taylor answered with only the slightest hesitation. "Sounds good to me, I will pick up my overnight case at your parents. That way we can go out to your house right after dinner."

This time Gabe disconnected. "Damn, I was hoping you'd stay at my place."

Taylor took her time answering him. She wasn't going to lie. She wanted to be with him. It would be another first for her. Going to sleep and waking up with a man, with Gabe. Her circle of friends and associates were older. When she was thirteen she had been shuffled off to an exclusive school in France. There were only six students and all were girls. The good thing was she had an incredible education on an accelerated timeline that made it possible to enroll in law school at eighteen. The bad thing was that she hadn't had a social life. She had never been to a movie with a boy, held hands, or snuck kisses in back seats. She had never 'parked' and made out. Of course she knew a lot of couples that lived together and weren't married but she had never been attracted to anyone enough to consider it. Gabe knew she had been a virgin but what would he think if he knew just how little experience she had?

Gabe waited for her to respond to him but she wasn't sure what to say. He finally broke the silence. "Why do I feel there's an elephant sitting in the truck with us?"

"Elephant?"

He laughed. "You haven't heard this, . . . uh whatever, said before? It means there's something big keeping us apart."

"Oh, well maybe a little elephant. I'm not sure what's happening with me. I've never felt like I do with you." The road was winding and he had to concentrate on driving, giving her a change to look her fill. His hands and arms looked strong in the dim light but she knew he was gentle with that strength. She tingled with awareness remembering the feel of them on her body.

His voice rolled over her, deep, reminding her of the whispered words he'd breathed when they were making love. "Good, I'm glad you haven't felt this way with anyone else because it's the same for me."

Again silence filled the cab of the truck. Taylor swallowed, her heart was racing and she fought the urge to take his hand like he'd earlier taken hers. As if reading her mind he brought her hand up to his mouth. She closed her eyes and let the feel of lips on her palm close over her.

* * * * *

Just short of home Gabe pulled over to the side of the road to give them one more private minute. The truck crunched gravel as it rolled to stop. With a shuddering breath he turned to Taylor. She looked at him and their gazes locked. He wanted to unbuckle their seatbelts and take up from where they had left off earlier.

She reached over and touched his face with the tips of her fingers. They felt cool against his heated flesh. He wanted to feel them on more than his face. He turned his head and brushed his lips across them. "I like it when you touch me. It's been so long, hell it's been forever."

"You must have loved Bonnie a lot. Will you ever love anyone like that again?"

He again caught her gaze. "It was different with Bonnie. She was always fragile. All she wanted was to be a mother and homemaker."

Taylor frowned. "And wife?"

"Yeah well that was part of the package but for her it was a sort of a necessary evil." He sat back and drew in a breath. He didn't want to talk about Bonnie or his marriage. A part of him would always care for the mother of his child but it had nothing to do with now, nothing to do with this amazingly passionate woman beside him.

Taylor looked like she wanted to say more but instead waited for him. Damn, he needed more time but Caroline and Eric would be waiting for them and Eric still had a long drive over the mountains in front of him. He pulled onto the main road and willed himself to relax. They were both tense and that wasn't good. Hoping to diffuse the situation he decided to bring what he wanted and was feeling out in the open. "I'm not going to lie or hedge, I want to spend the night with you. And, even though we probably need to talk, that's not what I have in mind."

If he'd hoped being up front would ease Taylor's tension he was wrong. If anything she looked more wary.

She wet her bottom lip with the tip of her tongue and Gabe bit back a groan. When she finally answered back, her voice was so low he had to concentrate to hear her over the road noise. "I don't want anyone to know."

"Know what, that we made love? Honey, no one is going to miss the sparks flying between us. Whether they take it to the next step or not . . . well it's no one's business."

"You don't understand. I came here to help Caroline with her wedding. I'm a guest at your parent's house. Mandy thinks I'm . . . well, princess material." She unbuckled her seat belt and moved over to the passenger seat. "Besides, at best we'd have this one night. Mandy will be home tomorrow and you and I both know we don't want her to see me in your bed or . . ."

Gabe knew she was right, besides hadn't he had the same concern about what would happen after tonight? This wasn't going to go anywhere. He was thinking like a . . . man in love. *Damn, where did that come from?* No one fell in love like that. It took years, years of getting to know someone. *Or did it?*

10

Taylor glanced at the dashboard clock, almost six o'clock. Both Caroline and Eric's cars were parked in the drive at the Lynch house. They must have been watching for them because almost immediately Eric came out of the house, pulling on his coat. "Caroline said to put the leaves and cedar in the barn. She cleared a spot and threw down a couple of old sheets on the floor."

A few minutes later Everett came out to help. Taylor had a load of branches in her arms. He took them from her and said, "The three of us guys can get this. Caroline said for you to come in and get your things for tonight."

At the kitchen door she paused, then opened it without knocking. She could hear Caroline and her mother in the living room. A pot of soup simmered on the stove. The house smelled of . . . home. Calling out, "Hello." She heard Caroline's voice ring out. "We're in here admiring the gifts that came today."

Taylor walked through the kitchen; away from Gabe she could gain some perspective. She had come to Washington to share this special time with her friend. Not to . . . She again tamped down her thoughts. At the door of the living room, she stopped. Caroline and her mother had arranged the corner of the room so that the gifts could be displayed and she saw that even in one day the number had grown considerably. Taylor joined the two women. "Wow, you may need a bigger house." She was kidding, she hadn't even seen Caroline and Eric's home.

Caroline's face was alight with happiness. It brought a hunger to Taylor. She wanted what her friend had. An image of what her wedding would be, of Frederick, of her father and how he would view gifts imposed itself over the scene in front of her. They would be lavish, given for political reasons, not from love like Caroline's. There wouldn't be a funny looking pig cookie jar or the pretty crocheted pot holders. No, her gifts would be silver, crystal, fine china.

The sound of the men coming in from outdoors jolted her out of her thoughts and Taylor turned with the other two women toward the kitchen. The weather had slid from Indian summer into winter during the day, and the scent of cold fresh air hung on the men's clothing. At the sight of Gabe with his sleeves pushed up, his mother went over, and smacked his upper arm. "No matter how old you are, you never dress for outdoors. Where is your coat?"

Gabe's laugh rang out and Eric's and his father's followed. "Come on Mom, there's a lady watching." His voice held a teasing tone.

His mothers echoed it. "Posh, Taylor's family."

Taylor felt tears and blinked them away. But not quick enough. A quick look at Gabe told her he'd seen them.

The moment passed and in a few minutes they were headed out to the car and trucks. Gabe hung back. "Sure you two don't want to come? We're just going into Scotty Bee's."

His mother shook her head. "You kids go on. Dad and I are going to have soup and relax for the evening. It might be one of the last one's until after the wedding."

Taylor followed Caroline out to the cars. Then remembering she hadn't gotten her overnight case, turned around, and bumped into Gabe. He steadied her. "Whoa, did you forget something?"

"Yes, my things for tonight."

Caroline and Eric were talking with their arms around each other and Taylor raised her voice so they would hear her. "Caroline, wait for me. I need to get my things."

The yard light was bright enough for Taylor to see Gabe's wink as his voice echoed behind hers. "It's okay; you guys go ahead and get started. I'll bring Taylor with me."

* * * * *

Gabe couldn't help the self-satisfied grin on his face. This couldn't have worked out better if he'd planned it. He watched as Taylor ran down the steps toward him and noted how different she looked with her hair hanging loose instead of the tightly coiled style it had been in when he had first seen her. A beautiful sight that made him draw in a breath. He reached for her night case and their fingers touched sending an arc of awareness through him. Opening the back door of the king cab, he tucked the case behind his seat and slid his hand to her waist while he opened the driver's door.

She didn't resist but immediately slid over the seat to the far side and reached for her seat belt. "Not going to sit by me." It wasn't a question, it hurt that she chose be on the other side of the truck.

When she looked over at him her eyes told him that she wasn't anymore immune to him then he was to her, and the hurt changed to concern. He let silence surround him for a second and then said, "It's too late. They know, maybe not the level of our relationship, but I'd bet they could feel the change."

Taylor closed her eyes and he got the impression she was trying to shut him out. He stopped the truck at the end of the drive and turned to face her. "Why Taylor, why do you want to throw what we have away?" He rubbed his hand over his eyes and tried to slow his heart.

Her voice was so low he had to lean closer to hear her. "What do we have? Physical attraction, will it be enough when we live a continent apart?"

He kept his voice as low as hers. It seemed a sacrilege to speak louder, almost like they were in some sacred place. He unbuckled his seat belt and reached over to unbuckle hers.

She watched his hand but didn't protest. Both released, he waited for her to make the next move. She drew in a deep breath and leaned toward him. That was all it took and he drew her into his arms. Whispering against her hair he tried to find the right words and finally let himself go and gave into what he was feeling. He claimed her mouth and she met him with the passion he'd begun to think he'd imagined. He ran his hands under her coat and his heart beat pounded harder when she drew back enough to give him better access. When she made a mewing sound, he answered with a masculine growl. "I love you." He hadn't meant to say the words but they were the essence of what was happening.

He pulled back and rested his forehead against hers. She was breathing as hard as he was and he waited so she would hear him. "I know it's too soon. Believe me if someone had told me it happens like this I'd have said they were watching too many movies or reading too many romance novels."

She gave a nervous little chuckle. "You don't even know me."

"And, you don't know me but all the same the impossible has happened, so the next question is what are we going to do about it?"

"Well to start with I do know you. Caroline loves you and she's shared her family freely with me. I've followed Mandy since that first picture of you holding her." Her voice faltered. "I even came to know Bonnie. She was beautiful Gabe. I cried when Caroline wrote me of your loss."

"It's been over three years. I'm not the same man I was then." He tipped her chin up with fingers to let her see his eyes so his next words would ring pure and true. "Taylor, what I have, what I feel with you is like nothing I've ever felt before. I want to know all about you. Not your past, but what you are now. What makes you happy, what makes you laugh, what excites you, and then I want to spend my life making sure you have all of that."

Gabe watched as tears welled up in her eyes and he pulled her back into his arms. "Don't cry, honey."

Her words were muffled against his chest. "I can't help it. I never thought I'd ever be where I am right now and I don't want to ever leave."

"You don't have to."

Taylor pulled back and as if on cue the phone rang. Gabe had left the truck running and Caroline's voice sounded loud over the Bluetooth in the cab. "Hey, where are you guys?"

Gabe touched Taylor's nose and smiled at her. "We'll be there in a few minutes. Order a Scotty burger for me and a cup of coffee. What are you having?"

"Well not one of those humungous burgers you and Eric inhale. I'm having a bacon cheeseburger."

Taylor chimed in with, "Order me the same thing and a diet Pepsi. And no comment on that diet thing, I like the taste better."

Caroline laughed. "Oh yeah, and I'm having one too."

Gabe slid back behind the wheel but Taylor didn't move from the far side of the seat. They drove in silence for a few minutes before he said, "I like you better over here. This seat has never seemed so big before."

"I know, but Gabe, I need time. All these feelings and, well, everything, is so different from my life in Manhattan."

Gabe pulled the truck into Scotty's and turned off the motor. He needed to slow down. Her words echoed in his mind. If he felt things were racing when he was on his home turf, what must Taylor be feeling? He opened his door and held out his hand for her. "Let's go get something to eat. You're right. We'll slow down, savor this time." With a laugh he added, "And, get this sister of mine married."

11

Taylor stepped into the restaurant/sports bar and stepped into another new world. Did they have establishments like this in Manhattan? No doubt, just not where she, or, more to the point, her father frequented.

Gabe's hand rested in the small of her back as he guided her down a wide hall toward the back of the building. "It's busy, not unusual for this place. Looks like a good thing Caroline and Eric got us a table."

Taylor drew in a breath at the scene before her. Booths lined the wall where a bank of windows overlooked what she guessed was the river. In the dark she couldn't be sure. She saw Caroline wave from the far end and changed course. With the noise level it didn't look like there was going to be a lot of conversation flowing. Caroline's eyes widened as they got closer. Gabe's sister hadn't missed his proprietary hand. Maybe noise was a good thing.

She slid into the corner booth and scooted around the back beside Caroline so Gabe could get in. He motioned over the room. "Can you believe this?"

Eric shook his head. "At least they're fast with the food. I want to get on the road and over the mountains. It looks like summer is finally giving it up. Did you feel the difference in the temps tonight?"

"Yeah, even in the short distance we drove toward the mountains where we got the leaves the change was apparent." He turned toward Taylor. "What about in Manhattan, are you getting winter weather there yet?"

"Not yet, but like here it will change soon."

The food arrived, and light, sometime teasing conversation flowed easily around the table in spite of the noise. Caroline had ordered Taylor sweet potato fries. Something she had never tried but found she loved them. Again she compared this life with the one she lived in Manhattan. Three days ago it would have felt strange, now it felt right. She'd told Gabe she needed time, but not to decide where she wanted to be. She already knew that somehow she'd found her place, in her heart she was a small town gal.

Gabe leaned in close to whisper. "Are you okay?"

She shook off the mood and turning her face up to his, whispered back. "I'm more than okay. I'm happy. For, I think, the first time in my life."

His gaze again held hers and the room with all the people receded until it felt like there were only the two of them. She held her breath wanting him to kiss her. He broke the spell when he lightly brushed a kiss across her forehead.

216

"If you keep looking at me like that . . ." He picked up his soda and took a long draw on the straw.

Seemingly unaware of the tension, Eric announced that he had to get on the road. Caroline started to scoot out of the booth behind him. "I'll walk you out."

"No, not that I wouldn't like that, but we both know it would take me a while to clear the parking lot if you come out with me." He gave her a kiss, threw some bills on the table and with a wave was out the door.

Caroline's voice sounded subdued but she managed a smile. "I always hate to see him off. I don't know how military wives stand it. For us it is never more than a week or two and this time only a couple of days. Holding a Sunday morning meeting is unusual even for his job but this time it works out well with everything we have going on."

Taylor could relate; all too soon she would be saying goodbye to Gabe. Her father had called while she was helping Caroline's mother this morning. He had made it clear that he expected her back right after the wedding. He was even sending the firm's private jet. She hadn't told Gabe yet but she needed to soon. With a high profile case opening ahead of schedule on the Monday after the wedding, her father had a point. Gabe's voice tore her thoughts away from her 'real' life in Manhattan. "I'm sorry. I didn't hear what you said."

"No wonder, you looked like you were a thousand miles away." He shifted in the booth, bringing her closer to him. "Actually Caroline and I were saying we needed to get out of here."

"Okay." She pulled her eyes away from Gabe's and met

the question mark in Caroline's. "I'm ready whenever you are. Do you have a lot you want to do tonight?"

"No, actually it's been a full day. And, we haven't really had much of chance to just talk. So, I thought we could get into our pajamas and have some girl time."

Gabe's laugh took the seriousness out of his words. "Girl time? Mm, I thought today's women didn't do 'girl' stuff."

Taylor was surprised he was giving in on her spending the night so easily. Then like so many times in her life, the voice of doubt whispered. *"Maybe he only said he loved you. Maybe he is having second thoughts. Maybe he doesn't really feel the things you do."* Caroline stood up breaking into her thoughts. "Give me a second to use the restroom and I'll be ready."

After she left Gabe leaned closer. "Don't even think it."

"How do you know what I'm thinking?"

"I see right through the face you put on for the rest of the world. And, I know when you're not with me. Like a little bit ago when it looked like you were in another world. I wanted to ask you where. Now that face of yours is telling me you think that I've changed my mind about taking you home with me." He closed his eyes for a second. "Honey, that's the farthest thing from the truth there is. Right now I'm fighting for control so I can do what you asked and give you time." He paused then added, "Just for the record, I don't need time. Taking this to the next level can't happen fast enough for me."

* * * * *

Caroline opened the door to the cute little rambler and

Taylor stepped inside. There were a few boxes sitting on the floor, but the furniture looked like it was all in the right spots. It didn't look like they had needed Gabe's help arranging it. Pictures sat against the wall waiting to be hung. Other than that, there didn't seem to be a whole lot left to do. "This is really nice. So what furniture had you wanted help with?"

"I still have some stuff in the garage to move. We feel lucky to get it. With the economy, it makes it easier for first time buyers like us to get more for their money. Still, we almost didn't qualify for the mortgage."

"I would have helped you."

Caroline held up her hand. "Thank you but I would never do that to our friendship. Besides, we could have bought a smaller house. It's just that Eric and I thought that with three bedrooms and two baths, this will be enough to start a family. Maybe even raise one here because it has an acre and a half and it's laid out in a way we could add a bonus room and maybe even another bedroom."

Taylor laughed. "How big of family are you planning."

"Two, three at the most but by the time you add in a couple of dogs, a cat and lots and lots of friends . . ."

Taylor got the picture and a twinge of envy again filled her. The image of what her life would be was in direct contrast. A huge penthouse, complete with maid and nanny and, if her first child was a boy, that would no doubt be all Frederick would want. But did it have to be that way? She knew the answer; no it didn't. All her life she'd tried to please her father, her mother not so much because she didn't seem to care. Now, seeing a real family, with real love, she made a decision. She wasn't going to sacrifice anymore of herself. She was going to go after the life she wanted. A weight seemed to lift from her, she felt . . . free.

Caroline's cell phone rang and she mouthed. "Eric."

Taylor shook her head. "I don't think so, he just left."

"I know, but he loves me." Caroline held up her finger to signal a minute and walked into the kitchen.

Again Taylor saw the sharp contrast, Eric had been gone just over an hour, and was calling Caroline. She had been in Laurelville three days and Frederick hadn't called her even once. Even more to the point, she didn't expect him too.

Caroline came back into the room smiling. "Sorry about that. It's snowing in the mountains." Picking up Taylor's suitcase she said, "Come on, let's get into our pajamas and have a good talk."

Taylor glanced at her watch. Nine o'clock, what was Gabe doing? Was he thinking of her? With a shake of her head she put on her slippers and made her way back to the living room. Caroline had poured wine and started the gas fireplace.

She knew Caroline had seen what was happening with her and Gabe and that Caroline had questions she was barely suppressing. Before she could voice them Taylor initiated the conversation. "So I'm curious, being a schoolteacher you have the whole summer off. Why did you plan an October wedding?"

"Eric. He works all year but being in forestry it's easier for him to get time off now. Still if I were on staff instead of substituting we probably would have had the wedding during school vacation. As it is, I'm not really taking time off, just not being available to fill in for other teachers."

"Do you want to get a permanent job teaching?"

"Yes, but this has been great. I'm certified to teach grades one through eight and I'm getting experience in all of them." Before Taylor could continue the line of conversation Caroline shook her forefinger at her and said, "Uh uh. No more dodging. What's going on with you and my brother?"

Taylor sat back and sipped her wine, letting Caroline stew for a bit. She'd known this was coming and was only surprised that Caroline had held off as long as she had. She had half expected Caroline would have cornered her in the car back at the restaurant. "What do you mean?"

"Ha, come on girlfriend, I would have to be blind not to catch the sparks shooting off the two of you almost from the start, but tonight. . . well you could hire out for the Fourth Of July."

Taylor chuckled. "You just have stars in your eyes. Right now I think you feel the whole wide world is in love."

"Nooooo, well maybe, but I think you and Gabe have something going." She grabbed Taylor's hand. "And, I think it's wonderful. You would be so perfect together." Her voice grew serious. "You know in the years we've been emailing you've never mentioned a man." She caught her lower lip in her teeth. "Well except for Frederick and you only told me about him last month. I still can't believe you want to marry someone twenty years older than you."

Years of New York society automatically kicked in and

before Taylor knew it she was covering up, presenting the 'right' façade. "Age doesn't matter Caroline. I've known Frederick for five years, he's a good man." She stopped and blinked back tears.

Caroline put her wine down on the coffee table and again reached for Taylor's hand. "Oh honey, I'm sorry. I must have read Gabe wrong. It's just he looked so happy and . . ."

Taylor reached for a tissue from the box on the end table. When she didn't reply Caroline quietly said, "So did I read you and Gabe wrong?"

Taylor hesitated, finally she said, "No."

Silence filled the room at the one word. Caroline looked confused. "Gabe's a good man. The best; and he deserves the best back, which I just happen to think is you. Don't you feel anything for him? Is that why you're sad?"

Taylor wiped her eyes. "No silly, I'm not sure why the tears. He wanted me to stay with him tonight and I . . ."

Caroline interrupted her. "Oh my heavens, and you didn't? Taylor it is so perfect. Gabe doesn't do casual relationships. If he asked you stay with him he really cares about you."

"He's your brother, how do you know he doesn't do . . . casual?"

Caroline shook her head. "I know. Modern dating and, well, stuff is different here in Laurelville. Or at least for Gabe and me and the people we grew up with. For us it isn't about sex."

Taylor watched as pink washed over her friend's face. Before she could say anything Caroline continued, "Not to say that sex isn't . . . uh good, great. But it's not the package. For Eric and me, and Gabe too, it's about laughing and teasing, and working together. It's about trusting and respecting."

She picked up her wine and sat back. "No Taylor, if Gabe wanted you to stay with him it was more than sex. Of that I'm absolutely positive." She laughed and almost bounced on her seat. "So, why are you here with me instead of with him, and don't tell me you aren't thinking the same thing because I can see you are."

"Seriously Caroline I am so confused. When I'm with Gabe it's like the world is magic. I feel things I've never even thought about. Maybe I should have read more romance novels and less of the classics. Or at least if I was going to read them, stay with Shakespeare."

Caroline walked into the kitchen and brought back the wine bottle. She topped off both of their glasses. "Love hits us that way. If I had thought about it at all I would have said there is no such thing as love at first sight. Anyway I would have until I met Eric. I told you about it."

Taylor nodded. "I remember and I so wanted to find the same thing. That night I dreamed of a future with someone I loved. Then the next morning at breakfast my father noticed that I was less then attentive to the business. He brought me back to real life with plans for me and Frederick and where he saw the future of the firm going."

"Oh Taylor, I'm so sorry. Why didn't you write and tell me."

"You wouldn't understand."

"Yes I would. Your life can't be that much different. You

live at home. Your parents love you . . ."

Taylor sighed. How could she make Caroline understand? "Don't get me wrong. I appreciate all the advantages I've had but did you ever see movies or read books with the plot of the poor little rich girl? That's sort of what it is like. I have every material thing that you can imagine. I would have money even if my father disowned me as I have a trust from my grandparents. I have an Ivy League education, I know that I live what some would say is a dream life."

She stopped and took another drink. Caroline shook her head and softly said, "But you're not happy are you?"

Taylor again blinked back tears. "No . . . and I try to be. I feel that if I could only make my father happy, be good enough, smart enough, successful enough."

Now Caroline's eyes filled with tears. "Oh Taylor, your father loves you. We've been friends for what, ten years. The things you write about your parents. You travel together, attend plays, and the opera, and . . ."

Taylor gave another heartfelt sigh. "Caroline, I have never been up into a forest and gathered leaves, I have never been to a regular movie theater, and I certainly have never eaten a hamburger and fries in a place like we were in tonight." She bit back saying she'd never done or felt what she had with Gabe.

"No but you've been to Europe, to the metropolitan opera and all those places you've emailed me. Maybe you need to socialize with people your own age more. Gabe and I love our parents and do a lot with them but our main social life is with our age group. From what I understand almost everything you do is business related. Even to entertainment. Do you even like opera?"

Taylor laughed. "You got me. Light opera is okay, but sitting through two hours of it is a bit much." She took another sip of wine. How had this sharing gotten around again to the purely material? It was more than that. She tried again. "I know I'm doing a horrible job of what I'm trying to say. It isn't about where I live, or what kind of car I drive or anything like that so much as it is finding meaning in it all."

Caroline said, "I do understand. I try to visualize what your life is all about and I think it's like understanding, say, a homeless person. Just in reverse. Still I don't think we'd be human if we didn't want more money, more things, more opportunities."

Again Taylor laughed. "You are so right; it's just that material things are the frosting on the cake, not the cake. Or for that matter the meat and potatoes of life." The wine was beginning to work its magic and she felt relaxed and maybe a little sleepy. She leaned her head back on the sofa. "I have started to make some life changes lately."

"You mentioned the free clinic?"

"Yes, and that was what started it. I may have taken up law to please my father but it must run in the genes because I really like it, plus I'm good at it. At the firm I do corporate law and working at the clinic I discovered I like family law better. It's a good feeling when you make a difference, see justice, and represent someone who deserves it." Taylor wasn't sure if it was the wine but she didn't usually talk this much, and certainly never about herself. She looked over at Caroline who didn't appear to be bored.

"So do you plan to keep working in the family practice?"

"I'm not sure but if I do it won't be full time anymore. You know we talked about money; well that is the good thing about having it. You can do what you want and make a difference without worrying about supporting yourself." She sighed "For that I feel humble, I didn't earn it so I for sure can't feel like a better person for having it."

Caroline mimicked Taylor and rested her head back. "What about Frederick?"

It was close to eleven o'clock but it felt good to be here with Caroline, to be able to talk and have someone really listen. Taylor's thoughts turned to Gabe. He had listened too. She shook her head and said, "Strange, but all of a sudden I know I'm not going to marry Frederick. What I am going to do is go back to Manhattan Saturday night and take care of the case I have going at the firm. Thankfully I don't have anything at the clinic right now. Then I'm going to get in the car and just drive."

Taylor's words got Caroline's attention and she sat up. "But I thought you were going to stay for a few days. And, what about G . . . ?"

"Gabe? Caroline, things don't happen this fast except in the movies or in books. He doesn't know me, how could he when I'm just beginning to know myself."

She glanced at her watch again. "We probably should think about getting to bed. You have a lot to do in the next few days and if we don't get to sleep we'll be worthless."

Caroline shook her head. "I could sit up all night. Or at least I could have, before we drank almost two bottles of wine."

"Good heavens. No wonder I'm blabbing my head off." Taylor smiled half to herself. Darn, she should have gotten Caroline talking about Gabe, this had been a perfect opportunity to learn more about him and she'd blown it. Oh well tomorrow, a new day, a new life and . . . new love.

12

Gabe looked at his watch . . . again. Nine o'clock, that was late enough to head over to Caroline's. His stomach rumbled reminding him he'd been up since five and the coffee he'd consumed without anything solid was beginning to send signals from his gut to his brain. Reminding himself to go slow, or at least slower than he'd started with Taylor, he grabbed his coat and headed out the door.

A fast stop at the bakery and he would arrive at Caroline's bearing gifts. He couldn't wait. It had been a long night.

At the thought of seeing Taylor his pulse sped up. Much like a moth to a flame he couldn't get close enough. On the trip to the woods he discovered her passion matched his and with it, a feeling of completeness, like all was well with his world.

He rapped lightly on the back door and waited. Surely they weren't still in bed. A few minutes later Caroline opened the door. "Holy cow, Sis, what did you guys do last night. You look . . ."

Caroline squinted up at him and put her hand over her eyes. "Come in quick so you don't let in the sun."

"Sun, you have to be kidding. If I'm not mistaken those are snow clouds in that sky."

She stepped aside and he immediately scanned the room for Taylor. Caroline might be hung over but she didn't miss much. "Unlike me she's been up for a couple of hours. Want some coffee?" She sniffed the air. "And what's that heavenly smell? Tell me you stopped by Wagner's bakery and I'll love you forever."

Gabe laughed. "You'll love me forever anyway." He turned to put the bakery sack on the counter and saw Taylor step into the room. He let his gaze slide over her, lingering on her mouth. She looked tired but she was still more beautiful than any woman he'd ever seen.

"Hi." She breathed.

He moved closer, it seemed the most natural thing in the world to put his hand on her waist and steer her toward the bar stool. He sat down next to her. "Hi yourself."

He heard Caroline clear her throat. Her voice seemed to come from a long way off. "Hey guys, I'm just going to run in and shower and get dressed." He nodded and smiled when she mumbled, "Not that you would notice I'm gone." Then raising her voice she said, "And Bro, you'd better not eat all the apple crunch ones in that sack."

Again he nodded and turned his attention fully on

Taylor. "You look amazing. I missed you last night. Feeling lonely has never happened to me before. So what do you think I need to do about it?"

She laughed and his pulse went into overdrive until he had to swallow to breath. He picked up her hand and traced his thumb over her palm. He wanted to kiss her and when she met his gaze he could see his need reflected in her eyes. He didn't need more of an invitation and lowered his mouth to hers.

He wanted her closer and stood pulling her against him, she felt so good. Soft against his hardness, he wanted more. He played his tongue across her lips inviting her to open up to him. When she did he sighed and entered heaven. "I promised myself I'd go slow." He exhaled, trying to gain control.

She melted tighter against him. "I dreamt of you, of this."

He pulled back enough to see her face. "I don't know what's happening to us but I don't want it to end." He kissed her again, but this time he held back. Caroline's kitchen wasn't the place to take them to the next level.

"Why aren't you at work? Is the clinic closed on Sundays?"

"Yes, except for being on call. And, it isn't my turn this weekend."

He settled back on the bar stool but kept her hand in his. "So getting back to you leaving, how long can you stay?"

She looked at their hands. He didn't like that she seemed to be avoiding looking straight at him. "I have to leave after the wedding."

"What time is your flight?"

She still kept her head down. "Late."

Caroline came around the corner and Gabe bit back a curse. He loved his sister but he wished it had been a longer shower. He was still trying to come to terms with how soon Taylor was leaving and he had more he wanted to say.

* * * * *

Thursday! Gabe couldn't believe how fast the days had rushed by. He wanted to stop time, but knew there was nothing he could do to even slow it down. He'd tried several times to talk Taylor into extending her time another week, then just another few days, anything but leaving right after the wedding. She remained adamant that she couldn't, even though she seemed to love being with him, and fit in well with the family and their friends. If he didn't know better, he'd swear she was born and raised in small town USA. When she went down to Wal-Mart with Caroline and came home with jeans, a tee, and a flannel shirt, the picture she made when she put them on was beautiful and complete.

Gabe finished up with his last patient. His aunt and uncle had arrived that morning. Beds were maxed out at his Mom and Dad's so they were staying with him. He loved them but if he could have it his way he'd opt to have Taylor staying over. He smiled to himself when he thought of his little ally, Mandy. She'd been pulling out all the stops to get Taylor to share her room.

He closed the door of the clinic and started across the drive to the house. The snow that had been threatening since Monday was still holding off. He hoped it would continue to do so until after Caroline and Eric took off on their honeymoon. After the wedding they were going to drive over the mountains to Seattle and take an early morning flight to Hawaii. He wished it was him and Taylor. They had managed to sneak some time in during the week. Not enough and he'd purposely kept things in control. He wanted her but it wasn't about sex. That they were extremely attracted to each other was a given, that they were physically compatible, well, it didn't get any better. But it was more. Taylor made him laugh. He enjoyed everything in his life more with her in it. He thought back to this morning when she had come down to the house with Caroline. Mandy woke up grumpy; she didn't want him to brush her hair, refused breakfast and looked like a little thunder cloud. Then Taylor and Caroline had walked in laughing and chattering away. Taylor took in the scene in a second and told Mandy to go get her hair brush. His little daughter had mumbled an "I'm sorry," and did an immediate turn around.

He smiled again thinking of it. Taylor would make a great mom, a great life partner and he wanted her for his wife. She hadn't mentioned her almost fiancé, Frederick, or Manhattan since their trip up the mountain. Could he ask her to change her life, give up the big city, her family, for him? If she wouldn't, could he move for her? Life! Well no one ever said it was easy. He put on his company smile expecting to see his aunt and uncle and opened the back door.

The smile broadened as he stepped into the kitchen and instead of seeing his relatives saw only Taylor at the counter. She smiled a hello and slowly stood up and walked toward him. He'd seen her everyday but it was rare to not have people around them. Finding his voice he said, "This is nice, I could come home to you like this everyday."

She looked nervous, a knot formed in his stomach. Closing the distance between them, he pulled her into his arms and lowered his mouth to hers. When a breathless sigh escaped from her lips he deepened the kiss. The world fell away as he moved his hands down her back. When she melted against his arousal he moaned. They hadn't been alone together for more than a few minutes since the trip to get the leaves.

He felt her hands push at his chest and it took him a few minutes to realize she wasn't physically with him, something was on her mind. Taking a deep breath, he struggled for control.

"Your mother knows."

Gabe couldn't get his brain to work, or at least the one that wasn't in his pants. That one was working just fine and was speaking louder than words. "Ummm." He mumbled and again lowered his mouth for more.

She turned her head so his mouth skimmed the side of her lips. "Wait, Gabe. Your mother knows about us."

"Knows what, honey? That I'm crazy in love with you? That I can hardly take my eyes or hands off you?" He laughed and followed her over to the bar stools. "All anyone has to do is look at us and they'd know we have something wonderful going on. "He held out his arms and said, "Come here, we don't have much time and . . ."

She shook her head. "We need to talk."

Ouch, this wasn't sounding good. "Oookaay, but can't

we do that, say when we walk back up to the folks' house?" Talk was good, and he wanted to cement where they were going, but dang, alone time didn't come their way easily and they could talk with other people around. What he had in mind they couldn't.

She traced his mouth with her fingers, then leaned in and sent them back to where he wanted to be. "I guess we can talk later."

He didn't need more of an invitation. He led and she followed until they were both breathing hard. He rested his forehead against hers. "I swore I wasn't going to make love to you until we made some kind of commitment, but it's turning out to be harder than I thought."

"For me too." She whispered back. "It has only been a week. You must think I . . ."

He pulled back and ran his gaze over her face until he caught hers. "I know better, even if I hadn't been first I wouldn't think anything like that. Nothing we did before matters. It's what we do after we found each other and I would trust you with my life." He stopped and kissed her lightly. "Understand?"

"Yes."

"Sure?"

She muffled a giggle against his chest. "Yes." She snuggled closer. "Yes, I'm sure."

With a low deep growl of need he again took her in his arms. She pulled back enough to reach the buttons on his shirt giving him access to hers.

"Let's get out of this kitchen." He walked over and locked the door. If his father came down, what would he think? With a chuckle he reached for Taylor's hand. Better to leave him thinking than for . . . "Come on, we could use the rest of the day and all night but that isn't going to happen."

Gabe resisted the urge to pick Taylor up and carry her up the stairs to his room. She was light enough it would be easy, but he sensed she needed to be in equal control.

* * * * *

Gabe rolled over on his back letting his arm stay under Taylor's head. He felt boneless, satiated and if a guy could glow, glowing. The weight on his arm eased and he slowly opened his eyes.

Taylor traced over his forehead with her lips. "Are you okay, what we did . . . are you hurt?" Concern echoed through her voice.

Hurt! They'd almost killed him, what a way to go. But hurt, not unless an extreme orgasm could kill a guy. "That was f---antastic, now you're going to have to marry me."

Tears welled up in her eyes. They'd gotten caught up in the moment, but it hadn't been rough, still she'd asked if he was hurt. Now she was scaring him.

She turned away and started to get up but he circled her waist with his arm and pulled her gently back to him. "Whoa, did I hurt you."

Her voice wobbled and a soft sob escaped. "Don't tease me?"

Tease that she was hurt? Or was it his raw comment? From what he'd learned over the past few days, most of her social life was around older people. And, he knew she wasn't used to intimacy. Hell he wasn't either, or at least not to this degree. "Honey, I'm sorry. What did I say that made you think I was teasing?"

A tear slid unchecked down her cheek and he wiped it off with his forefinger. Then followed it with a kiss that trailed down to her mouth. "Come on, if you don't tell me I'm going to think we were too fast or . . ."

Taylor shook her head. "No, not too fast. I'm sorry it's just me. Thinking about leaving, I guess I'm just taking things too seriously."

Gabe frowned. What things? "You're going to have to help me out a little here. Do you think I'm not taking us seriously?"

She turned away and this time made it off the bed. "We need to get dressed. You mother is going to wonder where we are."

"Well that's too damn bad because I don't want to leave until you explain how we went from a hundred miles an hour to zero in ten seconds."

Taylor grabbed a throw off the chair by the bed and started for the bathroom. He could barely hear her words. "I'm just being silly. It's okay, get dressed." The bathroom door shut with a distinct click.

Now what? For the life of him Gabe couldn't figure why the abrupt change of mood. It had to be something he'd said, or done. No, not something he'd done because he knew they'd been together on the action. He smiled at the term action as visions of their lovemaking restored his good mood.

Shaking his head, he got up and pulled on his clothes. Whatever had Taylor upset he'd fix. That settled in his mind, he freshened up in the other bathroom and made his way downstairs.

By the time Taylor came down he was ready for that talk. "I called Mom and told her we'd be up later. As you can guess she was fine with it and said to take our time."

Taylor opened the conversation again surprising him. "About what I said, how I acted. I'm sorry. It was nothing. I just overreacted." She came over to him and gave him a light kiss. Blowing the incident off she said, "Now, how about a cup of that coffee?"

Gabe took a couple of cups down from the cabinet and wondered what he should do. Taylor seemed happy, and back to herself. He could let it go, maybe pick up from where they'd been before he upset her with something. No, it was the something that was bothering him as much as having her upset. Granted they didn't know one another well but from what he did know, and more from what he felt, this was out of character for her.

He poured the coffee and handed Taylor a cup. "I know, this might be better left alone but I can't. I don't want to ever do anything that makes you unhappy, and more, that makes you cry. I . . ."

Taylor interrupted, "You didn't Gabe, it was me and I've got my head straight now. Please, let's just pretend it didn't happen. I'm so sorry I spoiled our time together."

Gabe leaned over the counter and took her hand. "First, you didn't ruin anything. Nothing, even a natural disaster could erase the feeling of being more alive than I've ever felt before. And, I plan to do everything I can to have more. To build memories with you." He paused and took a drink of coffee.

Taylor's smile had vanished and again he debated if it would be better to let it go. He was just about to do just that when she said, "It was just when you made fun of having to marry me. It hit a soft place I guess. I've just begun to take charge of my life. It isn't that I'm unhappy with how I live so much as . . ." She stopped and looked down at where Gabe held her hand.

Before he could say anything, she went on to explain. "It's kind of like when you're hungry for something and don't know what it is. You look in the fridge and cabinets and get this and that but it doesn't satisfy you. Even when you are full you still crave something."

Gabe nodded. "I know how you feel. I think everyone has cravings, maybe just not for something other than food."

She looked up and met his eyes. "I found a big part of what I was looking for when I started working at the legal clinic. And, then again when I got here, the town, your family, it was like I was home."

He hated to ask but said, "What about Frederick? Does he figure in your future?"

She looked angry for a minute. "No, and to be honest I don't think he ever was. I'd put off announcing our engagement because I think subconsciously I knew we weren't going to get married. Truth be told, Frederick no doubt feels the same way. He's a great guy and on a fast track with the firm so I'm sure our engagement is more of a business arrangement for him."

"That's why you're angry?"

The atmosphere noticeably cooled, Gabe didn't like it but before he could say anything she took her hand out of his and with a sigh of resignation said, "It hurts to think you would tease me about marriage and then to have you ask about Frederick after . . ." Taylor took his empty cup and hers to the sink. With her back to him he couldn't see her face but her words were clear enough. "I guess I'm pretty naïve. I guess I expected a 'will you marry me' instead of 'now you have to marry me'. I know you were teasing, but it's clear that . . . well, that I took you too seriously. That it didn't mean to you, what it did to me."

Gabe shot off the stool and around the counter but she held up her hand and stepped back, a warning not to touch her. Well damn, now he was getting angry. "Whoa, by 'it' you mean making love and it meant as much or more to me. Further more, I don't do casual sex." He ran his hand through his hair in frustration. "Cripes, Taylor, it's been way over three years . . ."

"Bonnie hasn't been gone . . ." Taylor gulped back a sob.

"Yeah, well she didn't like the wife part of marriage." He held out his hands. "I don't want to talk about Bonnie. Come on honey, we are way off base here." This time she let him take her in his arms and with a sigh of relief he hugged her to him.

He resisted kissing her; it wouldn't stop at that and it wasn't the physical part of their relationship that they needed to talk about. No, physically they were healthy to the point of being . . . of being. At the thought, he made himself focus on this rare opportunity to talk. It was

Thursday afternoon and by Saturday night she would be leaving and a continent would separate them. "Let's get back to where you were talking about making life changes. Would you consider a small town?" He held his breath waiting for her reply.

"I hadn't, in fact when I left home it was all just a slight niggling idea that I needed to find something. It wasn't until I got here that everything sort of fell into place. But I don't want you to think I'm asking you for anything. That just because I . . . we. . . "

She broke off and a flush tinged her cheeks. Gabe loved it. His heart had started beating faster. Yes! He wanted to shout "Honey, ask" but instead tamped it down. "You don't have to ask anything, having you here would be a dream." He stared down into her face and whispered. "I thought I was going to have to move to Manhattan."

Taylor threw her arms around his neck, then drew back and kissed him hard. Before he could react she put her hands on his face and said, "You'd do that? You'd actually move east, leave your family, move Mandy? For me?"

Gabe's heart was racing. "For us. For all of us Taylor."

13

Gabe whistled as he fought the tie on his tux shirt. Thursday night had signaled a turning point with Taylor and they'd spent every minute they could manage, planning, discussing and . . . well whatever. The whatever brought a smile to his face. The way it stood was that she was going to fly out tonight, take care of the case she was working on, turn in her resignation, and then he'd fly back there and get her. She'd protested him coming to New York but he wanted to meet her parents and formally ask their blessing on their marriage. He hoped that she would agree to a short, really short, engagement. Moving in together wasn't his first choice and not only because of Mandy.

He heard a curse from the next room and laughed. Eric! The men were getting dressed at his place while the women were doing their thing at his parents. He started for the door, but stopped when he heard his father's voice. It had been utter chaos the past couple of days. He glanced at his watch, half an hour, it felt good to be in the quiet room. A vision of Taylor settled in his head. He had caught a look at the dress she would be wearing and knew that while everyone had their eyes on the bride, his would be on the maid of honor. When the time came, and hopefully not far in the future, would Taylor want a big wedding? Probably, and most likely in Manhattan. Caroline had said Taylor was wealthy but other than the car she'd rented, and maybe her clothes, he didn't pick up anything that set her apart. She fit in with all the family and even his best friend, Pete and his wife. They'd had dinner with his friends the night before. Taylor had joined in the conversation with ease. If he hadn't known better he would have thought she'd known them for years. When they had said good night, Pete had pulled him aside and told him that Taylor was a keeper and not to screw it up.

A rap on the door and his father stepped inside. "Hiding out?"

"How did you guess? Seriously, I would say I will be glad when this is over, but when it is, I'll be putting Taylor on a plane and that I don't even want to think about."

His dad crossed over the carpet and sat on the edge of the bed. "You could go with her. You've got people at the clinic; they can handle things for a few weeks."

Gabe felt hope surface, making his heart race. He hated even the thought of letting Taylor go. Then reality set in and he instinctively knew he needed to give her the time she needed. And, she could do it faster without him. "You and Mom are the greatest."

"We just want to see you happy and I have to tell you, I'm not sure I've seen you happier. They say there's a special someone for everyone and I believe it. I also believe that you grab her when you see her."

Gabe laughed. "You are so right and I intend to. Things have been so crazy and I haven't had a chance to talk to you. The plan is for Taylor to get a current high profile court case she is working on resolved, and then I'll fly back, help her get packed and bring her home." He liked the way the words "Taylor" and "home" sounded together. When his dad nodded he knew that he'd caught the feel too.

A few seconds later another knock on the door signaled the end of quiet.

* * * * *

Taylor peeked through door, and whispered back to Caroline. "You sure you don't want to make a run for it."

Caroline giggled and shook her head.

Mandy came rushing up to have the flower in her hair checked and Taylor smiled down at her.

Bridget, the wedding coordinator came in the side door and nodded at Taylor and Caroline. It was time. Taylor positioned Mandy in front of her and watched as the double doors opened. The long aisle stretched in front of them and at the end Eric and Gabe stood at the altar waiting. The notes of How Beautiful swelled and Taylor blinked back tears. The song was perfect. The church, the colors, the people, it was all so beautiful. Caroline had chosen a small wedding party with only Taylor as Maid of honor and Mandy as flower girl. She had explained that Eric wasn't from here and the hassle of tuxes for friends living hundreds of miles away wasn't how they wanted them to spend their money. They would rather their friends use their resources to attend the wedding. From the looks of the church, they had; it was filled with happy faces.

Taylor watched Mandy step down the short step to the aisle and at the designated signal she followed. Immediately her gaze found Gabe's; she followed it to the front of the church and took her place.

After a few seconds of silence, the first notes of the traditional wedding march sounded. Taylor swallowed and tore her gaze from Gabe's. Caroline's gown was just the right style for her, a full skirt with hundreds of seed pearls gave it a translucent sheen as she moved down the autumn colored aisle. Eric stepped forward and took her hand. They had dispensed with the giving of the bride. Caroline's father had said they were gaining a son, not giving away a daughter.

Taylor watched Caroline and Eric say their vows to each other. Tenderness and love was evident in their words and touch. Glancing over she saw Gabe was as affected as she was. She felt a pull toward him as they shared the emotion of the service. How was she going to leave him tonight? It might only be for a few weeks but right now it felt like forever. An uneasy feeling fell over her. It was all so perfect. Too perfect. If Gabe asked her to elope with him she knew she wouldn't hesitate for a second.

The afternoon swept past with laughter, tears, well wishes and all the ceremony of love. Then it was over, and

Taylor was in the upper room of the church putting on a severe black pants suit, while the others were finishing the last of packing gifts and cleaning up. Without thinking she pulled her hair back in the tight twist that she always wore, or at least had until a few days ago. Taking a last look in the mirror she let out an "ugh" and pulled the clip out letting her hair cascade down over her shoulders. Opening the first three buttons of the tailored shirt, she grimaced; still not the look she wanted, but it would have to do.

Lillian and Everett were waiting for her when she walked down the stairs. She handed her dress to Bridget, Caroline's friend who had done such a beautiful job of coordinating the wedding. "We'll put it in Caroline's old room until you get back." Lillian stepped up and gave her a hug. Everett followed his wife. "Hurry back darlin', we're going to miss you."

Gabe came in the door in a burst of cold air. "That's the last load." Taking Taylor's arm he moved her toward the door.

Gabe and Taylor had taken her car to the airport that morning where her father had arranged for someone to pick it up and return it to the rental in Seattle.

It was cold and Gabe put his arm around her as they walked to the truck. "Want to know what I'm thinking?"

She nodded, though in the dark it was doubtful he could see. "Is it good?"

He opened the door and the light from the cab showed her his face. It didn't look like his thoughts were good. His eyes slid over her. "You look different, like you're already distancing yourself. Tell me that's not what you are doing,

Taylor."

"It's the clothes. When I left Manhattan, I went to the airport straight from work. This is what I had on."

Taylor grabbed the steering wheel and pulled herself up. She took advantage of the height of her position to lean down and press her mouth to his. His hands immediately circled her waist and he angled his mouth to deepen the kiss. He had parked the truck toward the back of the parking lot but the overhead light took away any privacy the location afforded them. He pulled away willing his breathing to slow enough to whisper, "How am I going to let you go?"

"It won't be for long. I'm not even really sure why my father feels I have to be there for this case. Most of the work I did on it was research and I left copious documentation." She bit back saying more. Saying that her father had uncanny intuitiveness and bringing her back to New York on his terms would be insurance against her deciding to stay longer.

Gabe released her waist and let her move over on the seat. "I wish now that I would have made arrangements to fly home with you."

"It would have been nice, but you would have been bored silly. This way I'll have everything at the office wrapped up and you can help me finish the packing and of course meet my parents." Saying the words she willed herself to believe them. She was too happy. Was it this that was giving her a niggling feeling that disaster was about to strike. It would help if Gabe would stop frowning.

* * * * *

The residents of Laurelville considered themselves

lucky to have an airport. Small, it was used primarily for crop dusters and commutes. It was late and the small terminal was closed but the tower was manned twenty four-seven. Gabe swung the truck up to the gate where a lone plane that looked like a Learjet to his untrained eye sat waiting. He let out a whistle. "Yours?"

Taylor looked uncomfortable, like she might be wishing she'd said goodbye at the church. "My father's."

Damn, Caroline had told them Taylor was wealthy, but this wasn't just wealthy, it was rich, like in 'Rich and Famous' rich. This was way more than he had bargained for. He wasn't a chauvinist. He didn't think it was the man's place to be the sole support but he wasn't about to be Mr. Taylor Hamilton either. Besides, wealth to a point was good, but rich, that was another thing all together. He gripped Taylor's upper arms and growled out. "Who are you? Why didn't you tell me you were filthy rich?"

Taylor stared at him. "I didn't think it would matter."

"Well it does. And, it's not a lifestyle I have any interest in." In her eyes he saw a wounded look and fought the urge to take her in his arms. It looked like she was holding her breath and then she turned and slowly walked up the stairs and into the plane.

Almost immediately the door closed and the plane rolled away from the gate. Gabe ran his hand over his chest. Now he knew the feeling of heartbreak. One part of him wanted to run down the runway and try to stop the plane, the other part wanted to get the hell out of there. Beyond tired he made his way back to the truck but sat watching until the plane was airborne and out of sight. In the short time he'd been there, ice had started to form on the windshield. Indian summer was over, and winter had arrived. He felt it's cold presence in his soul as he turned the truck toward home.

Gabe woke to sound of laughter and the smell of coffee. His Aunt and Uncle and it sounded like his father. Groaning he levered himself off the couch in his office. When he'd come in from the airport he had been too wired to sleep and, instead of trying, had searched the Internet for the Hamilton's of New York. He'd hit pay dirt right away. Articles, many with pictures, showed the family made the social scene on a regular schedule. Reports chronicled the elite family, the firm and their charity ventures. Funny that Taylor hadn't mentioned the charities they supported when she'd talked about the legal clinic that she was part of.

Right now he felt like a masochist for staying up until the wee hours of the morning. He hadn't needed more than a couple of sites and articles to solidly confirm what he knew before he had started looking. Taylor was out of his league, way out of his league. So why keep inflicting pain on himself? Why look at pictures of the elegantly clad Taylor on the arm of a guy that looked like he had just stepped off the pages of GQ? Granted he was, or looked to be, her senior by a couple of decades. Still, they made a stunning couple.

A burst of laughter thankfully pulled him away from the images in his head. "Time to move on," he mumbled as he made his way to the kitchen, the coffee and his family.

As soon as he stood nausea hit him. He leaned against the doorframe and willed it away. *Damn how long was it going to be before this empty sick feeling in the pit of his stomach went away? And, how long was it going to take him to forget?*

14

Taylor walked into Hamilton and Associates. Instead of working on the case records waiting on board for her perusal, she had used the flight to think through her life and where she wanted it to go. If nothing else this trip had cleared her head of its fantasy notions. Her father didn't do anything that didn't benefit the firm first and therefore himself. And, no matter how 'good' she was, no matter how much she tried, he wasn't going to love her anymore than he did. And that she'd finally realized just wasn't enough.

As for Gabe, she would think about him later. When she wasn't raw with hurt, when she could think about him without seeing the look on his face when he had realized she wasn't who he thought she was.

Her heels clicked across the slate of the outer reception area and she nodded to the receptionist who smiled and said, "Good morning Ms. Hamilton and welcome back." It was Sunday, but it wasn't unusual for staff to be working. Her father paid well and demanded above the usual hours.

Taylor took a breath and pushed open the leaded glass door into the inner offices of her father and the partners. His executive secretary greeted her with a curt. "Your father is waiting for you."

Taylor was beyond tired. Usually, she could manage a few hours of sleep on flights, but not this time. The look on Gabe's face haunted her. At first she had been hurt by his almost instant rejection, but when she saw again the look on his face it changed to guilt. Had she misled him? Not intentionally, but the lawyer in her looked at the situation from all sides and she had to admit he had a point. He hadn't had a full picture of who she was.

Squaring her shoulders, she opened her father's door and stepped inside to a world of opulence. The room was decorated in a masculine burgundy and dark forest green, with massive cherry wood furniture. It didn't invite warmth, nor did her father with his nod in her direction. Frederick was seated in a chair to the front side and he immediately rose and crossed over to her. "Welcome back, my dear." He buzzed her cheek with his lips. "I missed you."

Taylor bit back a comment. Missed her. She thought of Eric, how he'd called Caroline every chance he got. If she was defining 'missing' it wouldn't be from Frederick's quietly spoken words. Well, that would change because, after this case, she was done. Her father might not realize what she contributed to the firm now but, not given to false modesty, she knew she was good at her job and she would be missed.

She put the folders from the plane on a side desk and took one of the other chairs. And waited. After what seemed longer than usual Theodore Hamilton said, "Do you want something to drink? He glanced at his watch. "Or perhaps something to eat? I can have Ms. . ."

Taylor took a pad out of her purse. "No father, nothing for me." She didn't apologize for being gone or offer any personal rhetoric on her trip. She saw herself with a new sight. Gone was the delusion of a loving family. She knew what one looked like now. The faster she completed her obligation to her pending work, which except for a few minor things was only this case, the sooner she could move on with her life.

Taylor was glad her father had the foresight to bring in the support staff. Between the three of them and the staff the day proved productive and by five thirty they were satisfied with the case. In fact, with what they had, there was an excellent chance that it might settle out of court. "Well that's that, then." Taylor stood and reached for the jacket she'd thrown over the arm of her chair.

Her father motioned her to sit back down. "Did your trip go as you had planned?"

Taylor nodded, work over, her father would relax with her now for a few minutes before dismissing her. It was a pattern she had grown accustomed too. He meant well, she loved him and always would. He was a product of the Hamilton family, a mold she had almost gotten swallowed up by.

She said, "Yes, it was a beautiful wedding. And, the Pacific Northwest is like a picture postcard." She glanced over at Frederick drawing him into the conversation. Now that her mind was made up she could afford to be gracious. "Have you been there?"

"No, at least no further than to change planes in Seattle. I'm glad you liked it." Frederick didn't add that maybe they would visit sometime, not that she expected him too.

Her father stood up signaling an end to the day. "You must be tired. Frederick and I were planning to have dinner, but we understand if you'd rather have an early night." Without waiting for her reply he reached for the phone and ordered the car for her.

"I'll walk you out." Frederick's voice was deep, almost as if he'd designed it to go with his image.

A few minutes later Taylor let herself into her apartment. It was part of the penthouse her parents owned, but was designed with a separate entrance as well as a connecting door to their rooms. No doubt the builder had originally intended it for live-in domestic help. She kicked off her shoes and walked toward the master bedroom. It felt cold but she knew from experience the temperature would read a comfortable seventy degrees. The cold didn't come from the lack of heat, more like it had just never felt like home. Her father had employed the same interior decorator for both units and it was done in ultra modern motif with a lot of black, white and chrome.

Her bags had been delivered from the airport and she rolled them back to the bedroom. Tina, the Hamilton housekeeper would unpack them. Strange how this life felt so normal here and so far out of the reality of

Laurelville, Washington. It felt almost like she was on another planet, certainly in another world. For a second doubts assailed her. Could she change, could she take control of her life, could she live without all the luxuries she took without giving them a thought?

Her cell rang. Glancing down she read, "Gabe Lynch". Taylor swallowed to ease the dryness in her throat and willed her heart to slow down. He had called. The vision of his face when he saw the plane, and got a glimpse of who he thought she was flitted through her mind again. She knew she needed to answer, had intended to call him after she'd taken a shower and gotten something to eat. Reluctantly, she laid the phone on the dressing table. Later, she would call him later. When she would be more prepared to hear him tell her she wasn't the woman he wanted. That she wouldn't fit in with his family, couldn't be the mother for Mandy or the family he wanted. Tears slowly welled up in her eyes and she angrily wiped them away.

With new resolve she tore off her clothes and stepped under the hot spray. Coming back on the plane, she had made the final decision. Even going it alone, she was going to make her life what she wanted. She would make a completely clean break even though it would mean giving up her position with the legal clinic. When she had added that task to the to-do list she was making, she had felt a painful wrench. Then she reminded herself that there was meaningful work anywhere she chose to settle.

Taylor again felt a qualm. She usually ate in her parent's place. Tina always had something ready to heat up. If she went over there, she could let her mother know she was back. With a sigh, she instead turned toward her own small kitchen. Tomorrow she would make a point of visiting with her mother . . . tomorrow.

She wasn't hungry but she knew she needed to get something before she made herself sick. When was the last time she had eaten? At the wedding, Gabe had pulled her aside and put a plate in her hand commanding her to eat. She smiled at the memory. When she again felt tears fighting to surface, she forced herself to turn on the TV. 60 Minutes was on, a show she usually enjoyed.

By the time the show ended Taylor was fighting to keep awake. She needed to call Gabe, if for no other reason than for the common courtesy of letting him know she had arrived safely. A knot formed in her stomach at the thought of hearing in his voice what she had seen in his face. It had clearly said, "You're not the woman for me."

Taking a breath she dialed his number. At the fourth ring she relaxed.

She started to hang up when his voice came over the line. "Hello." How could just one word sound so . . . so wonderful?

"Gabe?" Like who else would it be? She fought to keep the tears at bay. She never cried.

Silence echoed over the line. Had he hung up? No, she could hear his breath then his voice. "It's okay, don't cry."

Her laugh sounded shaky even to her. "How do you know I was almost crying?"

"Almost?"

Taylor could see him in her mind, sprawled out on the bed, maybe with his shirt off or open? His presence filled the room and she closed her eyes savoring it.

"Did you go into the office?"

"Right from the airport, we worked until almost six. With what we put together I won't be surprised to see the case settle out of court. Tomorrow will be interesting no matter which way it goes."

"What does that mean to you?"

Taylor caught the 'you' instead of the 'us' right away. Gabe was being a friend, courteous, supportive, just not a . . . lover. Why, how could he go from hot to cold so fast? Again the image of Gabe's face when he realized the plane belonged to her father imposed itself. She swallowed and willed herself to answer. "I haven't fully thought it through yet."

Silence again. Taylor closed her eyes and gripped the phone. If Gabe wasn't going to lay it out then she would. "Look, I saw your face at the airport. To be honest I put off talking to you because I don't want to hear what I know you're going to say."

"And, just what do you think I'm going to say. Because just as honestly Taylor, I don't have a clue myself. After I left you last night I came back and did some research on Taylor Hamilton. To say . . . well to say I wasn't prepared for just how rich you are would be an understatement. We talked about how different our lives are, we talked about big cities versus small towns, we talked about your career. Hell, Taylor we talked about everything but the fact that there is no way I could ever give you what you have now."

Anger, foreign and fierce, surged through her. All her life she'd been warned about being cautious about people ingratiating themselves for her money. Men would want her for her money, her father had said. Now the one man that money meant nothing to was telling her that her money was everything. Except ironically it all was in reverse. Instead of wanting her for her money, he didn't want her because of it.

"Gabe, you are a snob of the worse kind. Only you don't clamor after the money, you run from it. And you stereotyped me without even giving me a chance. I can see now I made a mistake, but rest assured the lessons you taught me . . ." Her voice caught. She couldn't finish and with a muffled, "goodbye," she hung up.

Taylor finally let the tears flow. She cried until exhausted, she fell asleep. Maybe the tears acted as a catharsis or maybe it was hearing Gabe tell her she wasn't good enough for him. Taylor woke up with a headache and a renewed resolve born of painful knowledge. All of her life she had looked for something that didn't exist, at least not for her. Unconditional love! Hah! Another fact had surfaced and that was, yes, she was going to make a life path change, but that it wasn't going to be so very different. She had been on her own her whole life. The only difference was that before she'd been trying to please her father. Now she would be living to please herself. No more performing arts, at least not exclusively. Instead she intended to see the new movie releases. She would make friends and be a part of the social life of where ever she chose to work. To do this she would pick a small town, one where people knew their neighbors. From there she would just let life flow, and someday maybe . . . maybe she would find love.

15

Three weeks later – mid November

"I simply don't understand dear, why can't you wait until after Thanksgiving."

Taylor sighed, it was easier to give in to her mother then feel guilty about not doing what she wanted. One more time, and she had to admit that this time was different because her mother wanted her to stay and spend time with her. Usually it was something like being nicer to Frederick. "Okay, but no fuss. Let's have an early dinner so Tina can go home to her family."

Her mother smiled. "That will work dear. Just you, me and your father."

Taylor didn't miss her mother's meaning, no Frederick. The last three weeks had been a series of ups and downs. It started with the case being settled, actually better then settled. After seeing the facts she had uncovered and with the threat of a counter suit, the party suing their client had withdrawn it. That same day she had insisted on talking to her father. He hadn't been happy about it and tried to put her off, but the new Taylor fired the opening shot when she had handed him her letter of resignation. After that his time miraculously freed up. He took her leaving the firm hard, but telling him she wasn't going to marry Frederick had him almost in cardiac arrest. After that telling him she was moving away from New York was easy.

The next three weeks would have been strained, but she avoided him. This Thanksgiving didn't promise to be a peaceful one.

She buzzed her mother's cheek and, still a little confused at her request to stay for Thanksgiving, headed back to her apartment. She had decided not to take any furniture. She hadn't picked it out and without knowing what kind of a house or apartment she was going to get or for sure where she was even going, it was more practical to start over. Another surprise in all of this was how little she had managed to accumulate in her twenty eight years. Outside of the designer gowns and outfits she wouldn't need there weren't even all that many clothes. Her car would be filled but she didn't have to store anything.

The phone was ringing and Taylor hurried over to catch it. Caroline's voice floated over the line bringing a smile to Taylor's lips. "Hi, I'm glad you're in."

Since getting back from her honeymoon Caroline had started phoning instead of relying solely on email. She wasn't fooling Taylor; she wanted to talk her into moving to Laurelville. Taylor had told her it was over with Gabe, that it had been a mistake, that they weren't compatible as a couple. Anything and everything except the whole truth. Today Caroline was checking to see when Taylor was going to start on the road.

"I have everything ready to go. Maybe an hour to pack the car and I can leave."

Caroline tuned in to Taylor's unspoken vibes said, "I'm hearing a but in there."

"Mother! Can you believe it? My whole life it's been like I'm almost invisible to her. Now, well ever since I told father my intentions, she has done a hundred and eighty degree turn around. I wouldn't be surprised to find her packed and ready to go with me. She pops in to my apartment a couple of times a day with 'let's have coffee'. And now she wants me to wait and have Thanksgiving with them."

Caroline laughed. "Ummm, you don't think she is working on getting you back with Frederick, do you?"

"No, it's something different. To be honest, I am beginning to like her. She's funny and supportive. I'm thinking we may end up friends. Anyway, if there's a chance at building a relationship with her I want to do my part, so the plan now is to leave the morning after Thanksgiving."

"And, you're still thinking Colorado? Is there anything I can say that would get you to give it a try here with us?"

Taylor had fielded this question many times and it never got easier. Laurelville would have been perfect before Gabe. As easy as she had found restructuring her life to be, the one thing that she couldn't seem to manage was turning off the 'love' button. You didn't just flip a switch and fall out of love. She still wasn't sure how it had happened so fast or even the why of it, but the fact remained, she was in love with Gabe.

She took a deep breath. "That you want me to live close to you means more than I can ever tell you." Taylor hesitated and then made a decision. Caroline needed to know more of the truth. This hedging around things was risking distancing them. "The truth is that unless Gabe really has me fooled it would be too hard on him and . . . well for me too. I know it was fast but I love him and if I believe what he said, he loves me too."

Caroline's excited squeal resounded out of the receiver. "I knew it, I just knew it. He's been like a wounded bear and I swear he's lost fifty pounds. So why . . I don't understand . . ."

Taylor wished she hadn't opened up. How did she explain what she didn't understand herself? She thought of and discarded the fact that maybe Gabe didn't really love her. Her heart told her that wasn't true and now hearing from Caroline that he was suffering confirmed it. "It's hard to explain, and maybe there isn't an explanation. Maybe different people love in different ways. Or maybe love is one thing and building a life with that person another. All I know is that, for Gabe, love has a price tag. Maybe in all the other ways, he can love unconditionally but not where money is concerned. To him, my being wealthy is a deal breaker."

"I don't understand." Caroline's voice sounded wobbly,

hesitant.

"I know, for you I'm just Taylor. You know me, and you still love me. Rich, poor or everything in between just isn't anything you care about. But for Gabe . . . I don't know Caroline. I've tried to reason it out and what I've come up with is that Gabe needs to take care of the people he loves. He may feel that because I have money, I don't need anything from him. What he doesn't realize is that love is priceless. You can't buy it, believe me I know. You can't bargain for it. And, what you and your family have makes you far richer than I can ever be."

"So tell him. Taylor, make him understand."

Taylor bit her lip. If only it was that easy. "I can't. For Gabe to understand and accept me for who I am and not for how much I have in a bank account, or that I have a million dollar education, or for any other material thing, he has to understand with his heart. I think I might be able to convince his intellect, but for how long? I want what you have. I want unconditional love, priceless love. Because only that kind of love is good enough for me, I deserve it. Everyone does."

Taylor took a deep breath. "Whew, bet that was more than you bargained for."

Caroline started to say something but Taylor stopped her. "It's okay, really. I've come to terms with everything and now I want to start the process of forgetting and moving forward to what promises to be a great life."

Taylor heard a door bang in the background and then Gabe's unmistakable voice floated over the phone. Before Caroline could do what Taylor knew she would, and hand the phone to him, she mumbled an "I'll let you go," and hung up.

It wasn't that she didn't want to talk to Gabe. He had fallen into the habit of phoning her around midnight, seven o'clock her time. Usually he did this a couple of times a week. They didn't talk about anything meaningful, though lately he had asked her about her impending trip. After her conversation with Caroline earlier, Taylor didn't expect a call and was surprised when at eight thirty the phone rang. Like before with Caroline, she made a decision. It was time to call a halt. From how Caroline had described Gabe's weight and temperament this weaning away wasn't working any better for him than it was for her. Taking a breath she picked up the phone.

"Hello, I wasn't expecting a call from you tonight."

"Oh, and how's that?"

"I thought maybe Caroline had filled you in on what's happening here."

His voice sounded deeper. She closed her eyes, willing away the feelings that wanted to wash over and through her.

"She did, but . . . we need to talk. Really talk."

"No Gabe, we don't. After I hung up this afternoon I gave our . . . situation some serious thought. I can't do this anymore. I accept how you feel, I don't need to understand it. I'm glad that you were honest with me and yourself, but I need to sever contact with you. I may never find what I want but I refuse to settle for less. Not again. Maybe there isn't unconditional love, love without a price tag out there for me, but I need to work on freeing myself so that if there is, I can be in a position to not only take it, but to return it in full measure."

"Taylor, honey, please don't give up on me. On us." Could his voice deepen, it seemed impossible and yet it did. How could it be a lovers tone without love?

"I can't. Gabe, I just can't. I'm sorry, I have to go." Taylor pressed the button disconnecting words she wanted to whisper to him. Words that came from a heart that felt like it was breaking.

* * * * *

Taylor was glad that Thanksgiving had been less than a week away when she agreed to stay. Still it seemed like it was forever. She flipped off the TV that was tuned to the Macy day parade. She always planned to go downtown and watch, but never had and now never would. Instead of invoking sadness for what she had chosen to miss, she felt a sense of excitement of where she was going. The car was packed, and she even had clothes laid out ready for the morning. Even the weather was cooperating with clear skies forecast.

Opening the door to her parent's apartment she breathed in the aroma of roasting turkey. Her stomach rumbled its appreciation and she was smiling as she found her mother in their great room. "I see you are watching the parade, too. I had it on, it's just about at the end."

Her mother returned her smile and patted the sofa beside her. "Sit down and finish it with me. I always intended to take you down to see it, but somehow just never did it."

"I was just thinking the same thing. How did we let so

many things slip through our fingers?"

Her mother sighed and picked up her hand. "I don't know, I wish . . ." She waved the words away. "You know what they say about wishes? But your leaving woke me up. If I'm so lucky as to be a grandmother I'm not going to waste a precious minute."

Taylor swallowed a lump in her throat. All she managed was a whisper. "I'll hold you to that."

Dinner was ready and her father still hadn't made an appearance. Squaring her shoulders, Taylor started toward his den. Just then Tina came in looking flustered or as much as the unflappable lady could look flustered. "There's a gentleman . . ."

"Right behind you." Gabe's voice finished for her.

Without thinking Taylor literally flung herself into his arms. Without a thought, all the tears she had shed were forgotten. He was here, really here. His chuckle echoed over her lips as he claimed her mouth. She couldn't breathe, couldn't think, it felt like she was melting into and becoming one with him.

He regained control first and laughing said, "I guess this means you missed me."

"Missed you? I should be smacking you, not kissing you."

"Agreed, but . . . oh honey how can I ever make this up to you?"

One look at him and she knew he had suffered as much as she had. He'd lost weight and there were shadows in his eyes that hadn't been there a month ago. "You can't, and you don't have to. Maybe it is even a good thing because now we know what it is like to be apart and we will take care of our love more for it."

Her mother cleared her throat. Surprisingly she looked like she had been expecting him. He held out his arms to her and she walked into them giving him a hug. Taylor had never seen her mother so spontaneous. At social functions everything was controlled. Her mother never did anything without weighing the impact to her image. To say this was out of character was an understatement. A few minutes later her father came out of the den and while much more reserved he shook Gabe's hand. Like her mother, he didn't seem surprised. "So are we about ready for dinner?"

Dinner conversation flowed freely. Even if it wasn't with the same warm teasing that the Lynch family enjoyed, Taylor was happy. Her parents admitted that they knew Gabe was coming and again Taylor was surprised. After dinner her father suggested they take their drinks in the great room. Gabe opened the conversation. He turned to her parents that unbelievably were sitting together on the sofa. "If Taylor will have me I want to marry her. I hope she will forgive me for taking so long to get my head around things and not want a long engagement." He cleared his voice. "We would like your blessings."

Taylor could hardly contain herself. Marry her? Short engagement? She heard the words as they slowly took on meaning. She reached for his hand and squeezed it. He smiled down at her and she felt the return pressure of his hand.

"I didn't bring a ring. I thought we might pick one out

together." He whispered.

"I think I may be able to take care of that." Her father got up from the sofa.

Oh no, here it comes, Father in control mode. She knew his tastes and they weren't hers. "No it's okay. We . . ."

"Nonsense." He directed a look at Gabe. "Taylor." He cleared his throat and tried again. "Well, she takes a great deal after my parents. She certainly didn't get her uh, her casual tastes from me or her mother."

"For heavens sakes, Theodore just go get them." At her mother's tone her father nodded and left the room.

Taylor wasn't sure what to say. The day was so out of the usual, her parents were out of the usual. Before she had to say anything her father was back and handed Gabe a ring box. "Her grandmother rarely wore jewelry and when she did it was pretty simple. By the time she married my grandfather the firm was in the third generation so these rings don't reflect a lack of monetary resources. However, I think they may be perfect for you and Taylor."

Taylor wished he wouldn't bring up money and bit her lip hoping whatever was in the box didn't ruin the day for Gabe. He must have felt some of what she was feeling because he slowly opened the box. His eyes widened and he held them out to her. Nestled together were two beautifully carved platinum wedding bands.

"Oh Dad." Not thinking she went over and hugged him. "These are beautiful and perfect. I love them." She swiped at a tear; darn was this going to start again.

Gabe looked shell shocked. Finally he said, "I don't

know what to say. Like Taylor, I love them." He held out his hand but her father ignored it and pulled him into an embrace.

Glancing over at her mother he said, "Just take better care of the love that goes with these rings than I have so far." He walked over to put his arm around his wife. "It's priceless."

16

Taylor walked into her apartment, and found herself immediately in Gabe's arms. "Dinner was great, your parents are great but . . ." His mouth covered hers.

Without thought she melted into him. Hungry turned to need as he deepened the kiss and moved his hands down her back to her hips. She could feel his arousal and lifted herself up so her feminine softness would cushion it.

He took a shuddering breath and lifted his head. "I was such a fool. How could I have risked loosing you?" He rested his forehead against hers. "We need to talk but I'm not sure I'm going to be able to . . ."

"Later, we'll talk later. I missed you, I love you and I need you." She barely had the words out and Gabe swung her up in his arms.

He laid her on the bed and followed her down. Taylor reached to pull him closer but he drew back. "Let's get out of these clothes first. The way I'm feeling, in a few second's clothes or no clothes, it won't matter."

Laughing she made fast work of hers and looked up to see he was ahead of her. Again he took her mouth with his. She let her body rule and merged into the kiss. Pure physical pleasure washed over and through her. She was where she belonged.

Time, the room, the world receded and all there was, was Gabe. His mouth traced a path down her neck, to her breasts and she realized the sounds filling the room were of her making. He moved slightly away and reached for the protection he'd laid out when he'd removed his pants. Then he was filling her. In perfect sync they climaxed together.

Gabe rolled over on his back and put his hands above his head. "I feel like shouting hallelujah. Give me a second and I'll be ready for more."

Taylor laughed, "You nut. We need to talk. Can we still leave tomorrow? And, did you really mean it when you said you wanted to marry me? And, can you drive back with me or do you have a return flight? And, . . ."

Gabe stopped her words by placing the tips of his fingers against her lips. "How, after that amazing . . ." He turned his head on the pillow and let his eyes tell her the rest.

"Have the energy? Is that what you were going to say?" She flopped over closer to him. "I feel energized, and I can't wait to get started on the rest of our lives."

Gabe laughed, hugged her to him and laughed harder. "We are going to have a wonderful life, my love. But I'm predicting there will never be a boring or dull minute."

The sky darkened to dusk and Taylor dozed in Gabe's arms. But only a little and then she leaned up on her arms. "So answer my questions."

"What questions?" He teased. Then gave in. "Okay, first we can leave whenever you want. I only booked a one way so now you'll have to give me a ride home."

Taylor gave him a quick kiss and said, "Tomorrow is a perfect day to start our trip." Then as an afterthought she added, "Besides the car is packed. All we need to do is take the smaller bag I have here, and your things down to the garage."

"Good, so tomorrow, when we wake up." He lifted his eyebrows. "If we even go to sleep."

Taylor tried to keep her voice from giving away the anxiety she was trying to hold back. Gabe had proposed or stated his intentions to her mother and father but what if . . . He had said he didn't want a long engagement but . . . She bit her lip.

Gabe watched, and reached over, releasing her lip with his finger. "Don't do that." His voice dropped and he whispered, "Will you marry me?"

"When?" She held her breath.

"As soon as possible. Do you want to hold it here in Manhattan?"

"No, and until lately, since mother and I have gotten closer, I wouldn't even have wanted to include my parents. Now . . . now I'd like to have a small ceremony. Maybe Christmas Eve, at your church? But with only a few people." She stopped, was she going too fast.

Gabe raised up and leaned over her. Giving her a light

kiss back he said, "Go on, I like where this is going."

"Well I thought your family, Pete and Georgia and we can invite my parents though I doubt they will come all that way. I don't want a traditional white gown and veil and no tux. If it's okay with you I'd like for Amanda to stand up beside us."

Gabe again kissed her, this time lingering a bit longer. "Where have you been all my life, how did I think you having money or not was important? I'm okay with it all now so if you're giving up a big wedding . . ."

She silenced him with her mouth over his. Slowly ending the kiss she said, "I'm not. This is who I am, not the daughter my father wanted, and for sure I wouldn't have been the wife Frederick wanted."

"I don't know about this Frederick guy, but I'm not sure you aren't exactly what your father wants. He looked proud of you today."

Taylor's heart lifted. "Do you think so? He was different."

"Honey, I'd lay odds on it and it is only going to get better. From what you have told me and more what you've told Caroline over the years, your father doesn't know any other way of life. We'll introduce him to ours."

He kissed her on the nose and swung off the bed. Seemingly unaffected by nudity he pulled his cell phone off the belt of his pants. "I need to call home, make sure everything's okay with Mandy and . . . tell them we are going to be taking our time coming home because we are on our honeymoon."

He put the phone on speaker and Taylor laughed as

everyone on the other end started speaking at once. As luck would have it Caroline and Eric were there so heard the news with everyone else. After the squeals of excitement died down Caroline scolded, "How could you guys get married without me, without us?"

Taylor laughed when Mandy chimed in sounding exactly like her aunt. "Yes Daddy, I wanted to see Taylor in her dress."

Taylor answered back. "You will, though I have to warn you it is going to be a Christmas dress, and you are going to have one to match. This way we'll be able to wear them all winter, whenever we go someplace special."

"So are you going to have two ceremonies then?" His mother asked.

Gabe put his arm around Taylor and pulled her closer. "No, just the one. We thought Christmas Eve. And, before you ask, we are just rearranging the tradition of having a honeymoon after the wedding and having it first. I always believed in eating dessert first, think of it that way."

They rang off amid tears, with everyone still talking at once. Gabe disconnected the call. "Happy?"

"More than I thought possible." Pushing him back on the bed she proceeded to show him 'happy'. He took her cue in seconds. This time they made long, satisfying, slow love. Afterward Taylor drifted off to sleep with visions of a Christmas tree, and wedding. She had changed her mind. The ceremony would be in Gabe's, and now her home. The tree would be lit, and a fire would be burning in the fireplace. Perfect.

Night gave way to morning and Gabe came back from taking their bags down to the car. Taylor handed him one of the travel mugs she had filled with coffee. He smiled his thanks and took a drink. Long dark lashes hid his eyes, but she knew that they turned a darker gray when he looked at her and a jolt of excitement shot through her body. The thought of a pre-wedding honeymoon, traveling cross country, stopping in out of the way places, it couldn't get better.

Quietly they let themselves out of the apartment. "I'll call Mom and Dad in a couple of hours to let them know we got off okay."

When they reached the underground garage, the building was starting to wake up. Again excitement surged through Taylor. This was it, she had everything she wanted, had ever wanted. Gabe slowly pulled the car out of the parking space and turned toward the entrance. As the headlights came around, the elevator door opened and her mother stood framed in the light. Taylor's heart beat faster. When her father stepped out behind her Mother, Taylor couldn't believe her eyes. In unison they lifted their hands to wave. Taylor blew them a kiss and then they were pulling out on the street to a cold, clear morning.

Gabe reached for her hand and gave it a squeeze. "Ready?"

Taylor squeezed back. "Ready!"

The line of the wedding ceremony played in her mind. *"For Richer, For Poorer."* She silently added, Forever Love, Priceless Love.

The End

ABOUT THE AUTHORS

Laurie Ryan and Lavada Dee are friends and fellow authors. Living in the Pacific NW, the beauty that surrounds them coupled with rainy days are conducive to both reading and writing. With the models of their families it's easy to create stories of love, family and a happy ending.

Visit Lavada at: http://lavadadee.com/
Visit Laurie at: http://www.laurieryanauthor.com/index.html

Made in the USA
Charleston, SC
02 September 2012